Seduced In Red

By

Chad Wannamaker

Disclaimer

This story is intended for adult readers only. It contains explicit sexual content and is written to entertain and arouse. If graphic depictions of sexual situations offend you, please do not continue. This is a work of fiction. All names, characters, places, and events are fictional or used fictitiously. Any resemblance to actual persons, living or dead, businesses, events, or locations is purely coincidental.

ISBN: 979-8-9954986-1-2

This is a work of fiction. Names, characters, places, businesses, events, and incidents are either products of the author's imagination or are used fictitiously. Any resemblance to actual persons, living or dead, or actual events is purely coincidental.

Any trademarks or brand names mentioned are the property of their respective owners and are used only for identification purposes.

Seduced in Red

Book One of the *Heat & Honor* Series

Where duty ends, desire begins.

Some bonds are sacred. Others are scorched.

Where loyalty is tested and love crosses the line.

Chapter 1

He was driving her crazy. Nine years of wanting that man. Nine years of admiring, loving, and aching for him in silence. It was miraculous that Amanda had lasted all these years without attempting something reckless. But her birthday was two days away, and this year, she wanted him as a present.

I know he's got some code, all that honor and loyalty crap, and yeah, he's friends with my dad, but I'm going to have him inside me before I blow out a single candle.

Amanda's mind drifted back nine years to the first time she laid her eyes on Chris Temple.

She was barely a teenager when her father hosted a backyard celebration for the end of SQT (SEAL Qualification Training). She hadn't known much about Navy SEALs then. She knew her dad hated BUD/S and that Chris, with his light brown eyes and striking smile, had stood out from the rest of the grunts like he didn't quite belong to anyone.

Whatever it is, it must be really hard, she thought at the time. The party was for everyone who completed training, as they wanted to spend it with family rather than at some random bar. Amanda's father, LT Jackson Branson, decided to keep everyone at his house. He knew the guys were ready to get wild and celebrate. He figured keeping them close by would prevent craziness. He respected the guys, and they respected him in return.

I can't believe how much noise they're making. My door and windows are closed, and it's still so fucking loud, Amanda thought to herself.

Eventually, the smell of the grilled food wafting through the creases of her window made her stomach grumble. The loud growl from her midsection beckoned her to go downstairs and eat.

As she headed downstairs, rounding the corner, she ran into him and bounced back. As she was on her way to meet the floor, he caught her in his arms before she completed the descent.

"Jesus, kid, I'm sorry! Are you okay?" Chris said in a deep voice.

Amanda looked up, slightly angry at first, but then she saw those perfect light brown eyes. He was much taller than she was. She felt his arms bulging with veins and muscles, but still soft and smooth to the touch. The smell of cedarwood and freshly grilled meat filled her lungs as she took a deep breath, still not speaking.

"Hey Amanda, you alright?" he repeated with a more soothing tone.

"Ye...yes, I'm fine," she managed to squeak out, slowly taking another deep breath and looking into his eyes.

She was entranced like a moth to a flame. Chris finally let her go as she regained her balance and stood upright.

She seems like a nice kid, probably gets it from LT, Chris thought to himself.

"Well, LT's been telling us a lot about you. Nice to finally meet you. Well, other than me knocking you off your feet," he said with a low-toned chuckle.

Amanda nervously laughed with him, "Yeah, almost huh."

She thought, what the hell has my dad been saying about me? I hope it's not some cute little kid crap. Amanda now felt even more nervous, staring up at Chris. Feeling somewhat embarrassed, she just smiled at him. After a few seconds, Chris said, "Hey, let's go outside and get some food."

"Uhh, okay. Sure," Amanda replied as they started walking toward the party.

The walk out of the house, to the lawn, was quiet.

"Hey LT, look who I found inside!" Chris yelled across the crowded lawn.

Amanda's dad stopped his conversation and looked at her with a wide smile. He motioned for them to come over. The two swiftly made their way through the crowd.

"Aye, LT, she's a cute kid. You're going to have to watch her. Lots of guys are going to be coming from every direction," one of the other graduates said with the most obnoxious laugh. He was slim and tall, around six feet four inches, with a fire-red buzz cut.

"Ohh man, don't I know it. Maybe the fact that my body is a trained weapon will help," LT said through a smile.

They all laughed, but Amanda didn't see what was so funny about it. She stood with an aggravated look on her face. All the guys were annoying her except Chris, the man that caught her in his arms and saved her from a fall. There was something about him that made her heart flutter. His rugged scent, great eyes, and chiseled body made her daydream.

Jackson reached out and pulled her in close to him. "Alright gentlemen, this lovely young lady is Amanda Rose Branson. And Amanda, this is Terry to the right, Jacob, Nick,

Darren here in the middle, and I guess you met Chris inside," LT said as he pointed out the guys.

She looked around at the five men as her father pointed them out. Terry was the tall, annoying redhead, and Jacob was a shorter guy with an intense look. He was stocky and full of muscles. Nick was of average size with horrible teeth and the bad breath that came with them. Darren was an attractive guy with a shaved head, smooth dark-brown skin, and beautiful teeth. But Chris...that was his name; he was the one that Amanda hungered for. He looked down at her and smiled again.

"My name is Chris Temple, but you can call me BT if you want," he told her.

"Uhh...okay if you say so," she said with a nervous smile. "Well dad I'm going to go grab some food, I'm starving. I was upstairs studying and didn't realize how hungry I was."

"Okay, well go grab a couple of plates there's plenty of food. We're going to take some shots over here," her dad replied with a loud laugh.

Chapter 2

"What about this one?" Amanda asked her friend Lori while they searched through Express.

"No, it's too long. You want him to fall all over you tonight, right? Then you need to go sexier. A little bit shorter and tighter, like this one," Lori answered as she handed Amanda a dress.

Amanda gave Lori a dagger look and whispered, "Shh," with clenched teeth. "I don't want everyone knowing what I'm doing. You know how people around here love to just tell my dad shit."

Lori rolled her eyes and continued to look through the racks.

"I found it!" Amanda yelled.

She had searched for the perfect thing to wear for over a month. She wanted everything to be perfect. It would be her first time, and she had waited for the perfect guy and time. That perfect guy for her was Chris, and the time was now.

It was a red-colored, soft cotton dress that tied around her neck and had a plunging neckline, displaying her perky large breasts. The soft material hugged her waist and full hips, stopping just above her midthigh.

She knew her father would disapprove of the dress, but, at this point, she was an adult.

"This dress has to work. It just has to. I've tried everything and he still hasn't made a move or said anything to me," Amanda said as she looked in the dressing room mirror.

Over the years, since first meeting Chris at the party, he would typically come to their house. He had become a regular part of the household. Amanda would wear leggings, short shorts, and thin t-shirts and bend over in front of him, but nothing worked. He would usually just glance at her, quickly smiling, and then turn his attention back to her dad or whatever game they were watching. She found it very frustrating.

Chris and LT were no longer on active duty and now had desk jobs. LT was home more, which meant that she could see Chris more often, as she lived at home while attending college.

"Aye, bitch...that is so hot! Damn, that looks amazing on you," Lori said with a smile.

"Yeah, this shit is hot. I want to fuck myself," Amanda laughed as she stared at herself in the mirror.

The red dress accented her pale-red freckled skin and blue eyes. Her nude Schutz Cadey-Lee high-heel sandals made her legs look amazing.

"I'm good with this one, let's go," said Amanda.

As they walked toward the register to pay, Lori chimed in with, "Operation get Chris in your guts is a go!" They both laughed.

Chapter 3

Jackson was allowed to use the ballroom on base to host Amanda's twenty-third birthday party. She was so excited. She and Lori invited most of their graduate class to her party. One of Lori's friend's older brothers came back home to DJ, and the place looked fantastic. There were champagne bottles for each table, tables were covered with sheer tablecloths, and centerpieces were created with ice cream cones filled with pink roses. The dance floor was polished, with balloons lining the ceiling and confetti on the sides. There was an open bar, with fried tequila shots as an appetizer, giant balloons on the floor that spelled out Amanda's name and age, and over in the corner was a selfie booth.

They also invited Chris, Darren, and Terry. Amanda had grown fond of the three over the past nine years. They all stayed in the Seal program together until Jackson and Chris left active duty. Darren was extremely friendly to her most of the time; she thought he might have had a slight crush on her.

But his crush was nothing like her obsession with Chris. He was on her mind most days and nights. She would find herself going to sleep and waking up thinking about Chris. She couldn't even count the times that she fingered her clit and moist pussy, thinking of him rubbing all over her body. She would massage her wet clit and stroke her fingers in and out of her pussy until her legs shook, and she came while screaming his name into a pillow.

Amanda wanted to wait until Chris was there before she made her grand entrance. She was the center of attention and felt like she belonged on her own reality show. There were many gifts on the gift table near the entrance, but the only gift she wanted was Chris inside of her. Amanda was sitting in the kitchen waiting for Lori to give her the signal to come out.

Lori burst through the kitchen doors, "He's here! So is your dad. But Amanda..." she said slowly.

"What?"

Lori shook her head from side to side. "Damn girl, he looks so fine! He's not in a suit or anything. Just a white-polo shirt jeans and some cream boots. Damn!"

Amanda immediately got wet. She didn't want this to happen so soon, but she could feel the dampness between her legs. Everything about that man drove her crazy. She was enamored with his voice, 6'3", Chiseled frame, laugh... everything. But then she snapped back to reality again.

"My dad. What the hell is he doing here so soon? I told him the wrong time just so Chris would get here before him and we could have a chance to talk alone," she said with a concerned shriek.

"I don't know, but they are all waiting on you. Come on we need to go," Lori said, practically dragging Amanda down the hall.

When Lori opened the ballroom doors, a flood of blue lights and music hit Amanda at once. The DJ dropped the beat and yelled into the mic, "There she is, looking fine as hell. Happy birthday, girl."

She was bombarded with her friends from school, all wishing her a happy birthday, hugging and kissing her. She mindlessly chatted with some of them while looking over their heads, searching for Chris. He was standing over in a corner, talking with her dad. Amanda was just about to excuse herself from the conversation with her friends when she noticed a tiny blonde woman in a short black dress saunter over to Chris. The woman lifted his arm and put it around her neck. Chris didn't stop to acknowledge her, but he didn't move his arm either. Amanda felt like she'd been punched in the stomach. She stood there, staring at them, almost in a trance.

"He had the nerve to bring some bitch to my birthday party. What the fuck is that about?" Amanda screamed to Lori as she turned.

The chatter ceased as the DJ put on a slow mix, and couples joined on the dance floor. Amanda walked to the side of the ballroom. She noticed several young guys staring at her and knew what they had on their minds. She knew the dress would work but wasn't worried about it working with them; they were peons compared to her burning desire for Chris. But now she would have to work even harder because he brought someone with him.

Jackson and Chris were still talking when Jackson turned around and was about to wave to her, but he looked and frowned. She knew why he had that look on his face, her dress. Even though Amanda was an adult, her dad always had something to say about her clothes. Chris turned to see what caught Jackson's attention. The smile slid right off Chris's face as Amanda walked toward them. His eyes scanned her body and clothing, or lack thereof, and she felt even more excited.

When she finally reached the party of three, she noticed out of the corner of her eye the blonde woman staring at her and glancing her over a few times. The woman looked like she was in her mid-20s, but it was hard to tell with how much makeup she wore. Her blonde hair was an obvious bottle job, done poorly, but her face was almost pretty. Amanda couldn't look Chris in the face just yet. She stared at her dad for a second. Jackson didn't like confrontation with her, especially in public, so she knew he wouldn't say anything right away about her dress. However, she would hear about it later.

"Hey baby girl, happy birthday," her dad said quietly.

"Thanks dad."

Amanda knew Chris's eyes were burning a hole through her and she would have to acknowledge him at some point. She took a deep breath and turned to him. His eyes were a glowing light brown. He looked so good to her. She had studied his face for years and knew every slight change in it; he was more excited to see her than he had ever been, and she could tell.

"Hey Amanda, happy birthday," he muttered through clenched teeth. He didn't bother introducing the woman, but she decided to chime in anyway.

"Yeah, happy birthday Missy. Twenty-three is a fun one. I had a lot of fun when I was twenty-three and still living on campus."

Amanda noticed Chris tense up and squeeze the woman's shoulders. Her mouth formed an 'Oh' like she was about to say ouch, but the expression on Chris's face shut her up.

"Thanks BT and...," Amanda searched for the woman's name with a look.

The woman looked up at Chris to see if he was going to say her name. But when she looked up, she noticed Chris hadn't taken his eyes off Amanda. Slowly turning her head back, she replied, "My name is April."

"... An April, thank you for coming out too." Amanda said with a slight smile.

The silence between the three was painfully uncomfortable. Jackson stared at some kids who were undoubtedly trying to steal the presents. April stared down at her dress and picked some imaginary piece of lint from it, and Chris continued to stare at Amanda. Amanda stared back, trying not to look away first, but she lost. She started to feel self-conscious and folded her hands over her chest, which was on display for everyone in the room. She was not going to let him make her feel bad on her special evening. If he only knew that she had worn that dress just for him so that he could tear it off of her later that night with his teeth. She decided to be bold at that moment, "BT, since it is my birthday, mind giving me the first dance?" Amanda said with a straight and stern face.

He stood there for a minute, not changing his face. April stared incredulously at Chris, and Jackson smiled awkwardly.

"Sure, let's do it," he muttered through tight lips and walked past Amanda to the center of the dance floor.

He stood there with his hands on his hips, his neck craned, looking up at the ceiling and waiting for her to follow him to the dance floor. She turned on her high heels and walked toward him. When she reached him, he stuck out his arms to grab her waist, and it was rougher than she had imagined, but the feel of him taking charge excited her. Chris wasn't looking at her but over her. She placed her arms around his neck and tried to get his attention, but he refused to look at her.

"I hope you're having a good time. The DJ is new, but—" was all she got out before he interrupted her.

"What are you doing?" Chris asked blankly. He was still looking over her head, but he was breathing rapidly through his nose.

Amanda wasn't sure how to respond. She knew he was talking about the dress and the way she was acting but decided to play dumb.

"What do you mean?"

"Don't fuck with me Amanda. You know damn well what I'm talking about. You embarrassed the hell out of your dad wearing this and parading in front of me." Chris said with an attitude.

"It's my party and I can do whatever the fuck I feel like—-" she stopped mid-sentence again, as he squeezed her waist with his strong hands. She had only seen him mad once before, it was a little scary, but it damn sure was a turn-on.

He finally stared down at her and flexed his jaw. His eyes burned with irritation, or maybe it was lust.

"No," she thought, "My eyes must be playing tricks on me. He doesn't want me that badly if he brought her with him."

Amanda saw his eyes briefly lowered to her breasts, and then slowly, they traced the line up to her neck, to her lips, then her eyes.

"Do you know what all the guys in that room are thinking? Do you know how you look wearing that dress?" he asked.

Amanda was so lost in his eyes that she failed to notice the malice tone oozing from his words. "No, what?" she managed to get out, still staring into his eyes. Chris leaned in close to her ear, and Amanda thought, "It's about to happen right now! I knew it!"

"They think she's easy, like a slut," he whispered into her ear.

That word, that fucking word, was like a bucket of cold water being doused on her. Amanda's mouth dropped open. She released her arms from around his neck and tried to push his shoulders away, but his grip tightened on her slightly. She could not believe he called her that. She felt her eyes glass over but refused to cry in front of him. She only wore this dress for him to want her, didn't he know that? Fucking asshole.

Chris leaned down again and whispered in her ear before she could pull away, "And you're not a slut; I'm not calling you one. I'm just saying that's what people will think." He stated it as a fact more than a question. She shook her head no but felt like she couldn't move any other parts of her body. The surprise, anger, and disappointment froze her in place.

"You're damn right I'm not, and who the hell are you to talk to me like that? I don't really care what other people think, this is my party. I'm an adult, and I will dress however I want and do whatever I want to. Do you understand me?" Amanda said, her glassy eyes still holding back her tears.

"Look I'm not trying to argue with you, I just don't want some guys getting the wrong impression because then I might have to kill someone." He said in a serious tone.

"Look I appreciate what you're trying to do, but don't ever come to a girl's birthday party and tell her she looks like a slut and expect anything nice to come from it. Your intentions don't matter, you're just being an asshole right now." Amanda said as she walked off to find her friends.

Chris was left stunned at what just occurred. He turned around and walked over to find April sitting in a chair, looking very bored and annoyed.

"How nice of you to come the fuck back? You done with the little first dance?"

"Yeah, we're done. Come on."

He grabbed her hand and walked toward the door. They stopped, and Chris said a few words to Amanda's dad. Chris shook his hand, and then they walked out. He left without so much as glancing back in Amanda's direction.

"Well, that was a huge bust! My party is officially over," Amanda thought to herself as the music was blasting and everyone else was having a great time.

Lori found her friend looking sad. She walked over to her and cautiously asked, "What happened, why are you so upset? Where's Chris?"

Amanda looked up at Lori, holding back the flood of tears that were eager to burst from the leavy of her eyes. "Fuck him, just...whatever," Amanda eked out just as her tears broke free from their bondage.

Lori sat down beside her friend, not verbalizing anything. She just held her hand and allowed her to cry as the party around the corner raged on without them. The lasting impression of the conversation with Chris weighed heavily on Amanda's mind as she remained in a sullen mood for the rest of the evening.

Chapter 4

"Ohh fuck, BT! Yes... fuck me harder... Ohh, Ohh, Ohh!" April screamed, while on all fours in the middle of his bed, with Chris fucking her from behind. He had her blonde hair in one hand and his other hand on her ass, squeezing hard. Chris's body was tense as he was planning to stroke her pussy into oblivion. He needed this release. His strong thrusts slamming into her ass cheeks were rocking her body to the fringes of the bed. Both were sweating and panting loudly. Chris was dripping sweat on April's back, and she was dripping on the bed. The sounds of squishing as his cock went in and out of her pussy sent them both to out-of-this-world pleasure. April was a natural squirter, and she soaked the entire bed.

"I love feeling you inside of me, BT! Do you like it? You like this tight pussy?" She screamed as she squirted again, filling the already-soaked bed with even more of her juices.

"Yeah, it's so tight," Chris replied with hurried breaths.

He didn't care if his dick would be sore after this; he was going to pound her long and hard. The bed slammed up against the wall with every thrust.

April screamed out, "Stick it in my ass!"

Chris acquiesced to her request, grabbing the lube out of the top drawer, squirting it onto his hand, fingering it into her asshole, then slamming his rod inside.

He had been trying to calm himself down since that stupid birthday party. He couldn't believe Amanda had worn that damn dress. When she walked, the dress barely covered her ass. She had the best ass he had ever seen. He's seen it before, but tonight was something different. If he were honest with himself, he began staring at it about two years ago. Amanda was about 5'4", with long, flowing dark-blonde hair, gorgeous blue eyes, pale skin with slight freckles, perky tits, and a juicy ass. The large, lensed aviator glasses she wore for fashion accentuated her beautiful eyes. She was driving him crazy. As soon as he saw Amanda at the party, he wanted to drag her out to his car and fuck her up against the hood. Chris had thoughts about fucking her before tonight, but nothing as vividly as what he experienced this night. He wanted to claim her body for the evening and have her claim his. And he knew all those young guys at the party were thinking about her too.

*****

Usually, in front of Jackson, Chris had always maintained a safe emotional distance from Amanda, never revealing an attraction to her. Chris had too much respect for her dad. Jackson had singlehandedly changed his life, and Chris often felt like he was the father he never had. Chris never knew his biological father. When he was six, his mother left him with his aunt Sybil one day and never returned. He lived with his aunt and uncle, Sybil and Harold until he was seventeen. The life they provided him was difficult and filled with abuse. Three years into his stay with Sybil and Harold, Harold started to physically abuse Chris. He would attack Chris with brooms, chairs, pans, and, in one instance, hot grease. Sybil would witness the abuse; she would make excuses for Harold's heinous actions.

One day after his seventeenth birthday, Chris came home from a lunch date with Elly. Harold was expecting him home an hour earlier.

"Hey boy, where the hell have you been?" Harold asked with the horrible stench of cheap beer steaming from his mouth.

"I had a date. I told you about..." was Chris could get out before Harold hit him in the face.

'Slap'

A stinging, definitive, open right hand came directly across Chris's temple.

"Wha...wha, what did you hit me for? I didn't do anything, and I told you where I was going." He said as he clutched the side of his head.

"Don't back talk me boy, I tell you what to do and you listen. This ain't a democracy."

"Do you even know how to spell that, Harold?"

'Whoosh,' Harold's hand came up to strike again, but Chris dodged the blow.

"I'm sick of you hitting me!" Chris screamed as he grabbed the closest thing to him and swung.

A loud reverberating 'gong,' sound echoed as the nonstick IMUSA frying pan crashed into Harold's forehead.

'Thud!' The deep sound of Harold's body hitting the floor made Sybil run into the kitchen.

"Ah! What did you do? Did you kill my husband you bastard!" Sybil screamed as she bent down to check on Harold. While wiping the blood from his gushing head wound, Sybil managed to gather herself and remembered that she needed to put pressure on a bleeding wound. She grabbed the kitchen towel and yelled at Chris to call an ambulance.

"Do something useful damn you. Call 911!"

Chris remained silent as he slowly grabbed the phone and called 911.

"Hello, what is the nature of your emergency?"

"My name is Chris, and I just hit my uncle in the head with a frying pan, for beating my ass for years," Chris said with a direct tone.

He looked down at his uncle's motionless body as the blood oozed from around the towel. The blood was not affecting him like he assumed it would. He actually felt calm seeing Harold bleed.

As the ambulance and police arrived, Chris calmly walked outside to tell them what happened.

"He been hitting me for years, but I wasn't taking that shit today. Today, I decided I had enough of that bastard hitting me," he calmly explained to the officer as the sunlight shined on his face.

The officer was quiet, and his face didn't give off what he was thinking. Luckily for Chris, the officer that he was giving his statement to lived in the neighborhood, and he had prior knowledge of the abuse.

"Listen, son, I know what was happening in that house. I just couldn't do anything about it. Without a complaint or direct evidence my hands were tied. Don't worry though, I'll write self-defense in the report and protect you as much as I can. Again, I'm so sorry I couldn't do anything sooner," the officer said with a look of relief.

The EMTs loaded Harold into the bus and took him to the nearest hospital. He was still breathing but unconscious when they arrived at the emergency department. Sybil rode with them and was still upset when they got Harold to his room.

"I want that bastard arrested for attempted murder!" she yelled to the officer outside of the hospital room.

"Ma'am, you need to calm down, okay. Now, I will not be arresting that young man right now. It appears that this was a case of self-defense," the officer stated with a stern look.

"How is hitting my husband with a frying pan anything but?"

"The fact that this young man has a busted lip and black eye tells me that something happened in that kitchen. And...forgive me ma'am but I know what happens in that house. I live two houses away and I can hear the violence." The anger building within the officer was filling his tone. "Now, I'm going to write this up as self-defense. Is there anything else I can do for you?"

"No, you damn cops are good for nothing anyway. Jus' leave n' take Chris's nasty ass with you. I don't want him in my house no mo.' When I get home, he best be gone or something bad is gonna to happen to him." Sybil said as she turned her back and walked into Harold's room.

Chris returned home with the help of two officers and got most of his stuff out of the house. His face was still throbbing and on fire from the slap. He was also somewhat embarrassed by the entire situation. True, this home had been hell, but it was a hell that he knew. He would now have to start over at a new place.

At the hospital, Sybil cursed him relentlessly and told him to his face that he had to get out. "Your mother should've aborted you and saved the world from your uselessness." That was the last statement that Chris heard from Sybil before he left the hospital.

Chris squatted at different houses after leaving his aunt and uncle when he couldn't couch surf with friends. He planned to drop out of school, but since he was almost done, he decided to stick it out and graduate.

At least now, with the diploma, I'll have something to show for all those years of hell. Maybe this will keep me from ever going through that again, he thought as he sat in the middle of an abandoned house. The hunger Chris felt at that moment was only exceeded by the sheer cold, as his body shivered. He fell asleep, wishing and thinking of better days to come.

After graduating from school, he got a job working part-time at Burger King. Chris absolutely hated his job. To him, it was one of the most demeaning jobs he could have, but they had flexible schedules, and he could eat for free most days. While working at Burger King, he met his friend Kevin. It was Kevin that came to him with an idea to make some extra money.

The Burger King parking lot smelled like fryer grease and asphalt baked too long in the sun. The evening air was thick and humid, the kind that clung to your skin. Chris leaned against the rusting dumpster, peeling the label off his half-empty Gatorade bottle. At the same time, Kevin paced a few steps away, flicking a cheap lighter open and closed. The steady 'sizzle' of the flame filled the silence between them.

Kevin stopped suddenly, looking up with that grin he always got when he was about to say something stupid. "You ever think about how we really out here bustin' our ass for chump change?"

Chris snorted. "Man, every damn day. But what else we supposed to do? Ain't like we got options."

"That's the problem," Kevin said, shaking his head. "We out here slavin' for minimum wage and some free fries, while dudes out there hustlin' making real money."

Chris shot him a look. "Real money gets you real jail time. You trying to be on the news, dumbass?"

"Nah, man. Not like that," Kevin said, waving him off. "I'm talkin' easy money. No risk, quick flips. Smart money."

Chris raised an eyebrow. "Smart money still sounds like some dumb shit."

Kevin stepped closer, his voice dropping like he was letting Chris in on a secret.

"You ever notice how people just hand over their keys to some random fuckin' dude in a vest at them fancy-ass restaurants? No questions, no nothing. Just assume he work there."

Chris frowned, arms crossing. "And?"

"And, what if that dude was us?" Kevin's grin widened. "What if we were the valets?"

Chris stared at him for a second, then let out a short laugh.

"You out of your damn mind."

Kevin ignored him. "Think about it. We get some vests, set up outside a club or hotel, wherever rich folks go. They pull up, hand us the keys, we drive off, and boom—easy money."

Chris shook his head. "And then what? You just gon' keep the car? What happens when they start looking for it? Plus, those fancy cars have trackers."

Kevin smirked. "I got a connect. Salvage yard guy. He takes the cars, strips 'em, flips 'em—no paper trail, no tracker, no heat. We in, we out, and we split the cash."

Chris exhaled, rubbing the back of his head. He wasn't stupid. He knew working at Burger King wasn't some temporary stop on the way to a better life. For him, it was a dead end. But this valet idea? This was a whole different road, and once he stepped on it, there was no turning back.

"This is some wild shit, Kev."

Kevin spread his arms. "Bitch, we dump trash and clean toilets at Burger King. We already at rock bottom. You really tryna be here forever?"

Chris hesitated. His gut told him to walk away, but his bank account told him otherwise.

"How much we are talkin'?"

Kevin grinned as he knew Chris would love the answer. "Depends on the car, but hundreds, sometimes thousands a pop."

Chris rubbed his chin, thinking. "How many times you thought this through?"

Kevin flicked the lighter again, the flame dancing between them before disappearing. "Man, I live off scheming. This the one."

Chris let out a slow breath, looking past Kevin at the empty lot, like the answer might be out there somewhere. But he already knew what he was going to say.

"Alright," Chris muttered. "Let's say I'm in. What's next?"

Kevin's grin stretched wider. "We get the vests."

From the proceeds of their illicit side job, Chris and Kevin got an apartment with each other. They would party, work at Burger King, and then, a couple of times a week, they would pull their valet scheme.

Eventually, Kevin's girlfriend, Nina, moved in. Chris didn't understand Kevin's attraction to Nina. He wasn't especially attracted to her, but she did have sex appeal. The conflict of not finding her attractive but sexy filled Chris with something. There was something about her that he found irresistibly seductive. Being a friend, Chris never acted on his feelings, but he had no idea that Nina felt the same way about him.

One day, while Kevin was at work, Nina made the first move. She got out of the shower and walked back to the bedroom.

"Hey Chris, will come grab something for me in the closest? I can't reach." She said from the cover of the room door.

"Yeah sure, but don't you want to get dressed first?" Chris called back from the living room.

"Ohh, I will after you grab the thing for me." She said with a sly smile.

Chris cautiously got up from the couch and walked into the room, making sure not to look her way.

"So, what is it you want me to grab?"

"I want you to grab this ass," she said as she let the large towel drop from her body to the floor.

It was at that moment that Chris decided, "You know what, why shouldn't I fuck her? I mean pussy is pussy, and it's not like they're married or anything," he thought as he began to lick Nina's neck.

Why should I care about people when no one cares about me. My bitch of an aunt and uncle don't care. My friends are all flaky, and if I'm not doing what they want, I'm sure I could just vanish from the face of the earth, and they wouldn't care. My father was never there for me and my mom left. My own mother decided that I wasn't worth her time. Kevin just wants to steal, get drunk, and act like life is just one giant party. This internal monologue continued in Chris's head as Nina's wet insides slid up and down his rock-hard cock.

"Ohh I'm going to cum!" Nina screamed as she creamed all over Chris's stomach.

"Uhh," he moaned as he blasted a load of cum into her at the same time.

Chapter 5

A FEW WEEKS LATER...

One random afternoon, after leaving from pleasuring Nina, Chris found himself standing at the bus stop, waiting on Kevin. The air was thick with humidity and clung to Chris's skin, making everything feel heavy. He glanced up just as a bus rolled out; its brakes hissed as it pulled away from the curb. There wasn't anything special about it, just another dented, dirty city bus, the usual. But it was the sign on the side that caught his eye.

BE ALL YOU CAN BE.

It was one of those Army recruitment posters, the kind you saw everywhere but never really paid attention to. The poster showcased a guy in uniform, standing tall, looking like he had his whole life figured out. Chris had never entertained the idea of the military before. Never once had he pictured himself in camo, marching in formation, and following orders.

"Hell no," he thought.

Chris knew his temper. There was no way he was about to let some assholes get in his face and tell him he was dirt. But in that same breath, another thought hit him. Atlanta was all he had ever known. The city had raised him, shaped him, and toughened him. But it had also damaged him, and most of that pain wasn't physical. It was the kind of weight that sat on his chest and made him feel like no matter how hard he ran, he wasn't ever really going anywhere.

Chris exhaled, rubbing the top of his head. "Maybe the Army is just another trap. Another lie.

Or maybe it's a way out."

He shrugged his shoulders and continued with his day.

Later that night, Chris was surfing through TV channels. Nina and Kevin were in their room going at it. He could hear her panting and screaming, much like he made her do. She was close to cumming, but Kevin blew his load too quickly. Chris smirked to himself as he heard Nina complaining about being left on the edge of pleasure. He stopped at a program on the Discovery Channel about Navy Seals.

Chris sat on the edge of his bed, eyes glued to the screen. The video played on a loop, men moving with precise, lethal grace, their bodies fluid yet controlled, executing techniques that looked damn near impossible. He watched them strike, counter, maneuver, their discipline evident in every motion. It looked hard as hell, but it also looked badass.

He exhaled sharply, running a hand over his jaw. That's what he wanted for his life now. No more wasting time in this town. No more waiting for something to change. If he wanted out, he had to take that first step himself.

A quick search led him to their training facility in California. That was all he needed to know.

Chris stood up; his decision was made in an instant. He grabbed his duffel bag from the closet and tossed in the essentials. It didn't take long because he didn't own much, and he sure as hell wasn't sentimental. A couple of shirts, a pair of jeans, some cash he had stashed away, and his old combat boots. That was it.

He paused for a moment in the living room as his gaze drifted toward Kevin's room. Kevin was the only person who'd ever really had his back. Chris knew Kevin hated it there just as much as he did, but whether he'd ever find the nerve to leave? That was another story.

He put his bag on the floor and grabbed a piece of paper. Chris scrawled a simple note:

Kev,

Hey, man, I'm out of here. If you ever get the urge to leave this shithole, look me up in California.

Peace.

BT.

He folded the note and set it on the table. No long goodbyes and no second thoughts. Chris slung the duffel over his shoulder, threw his key on the table, took one last look around the place that had never really felt like home, and walked out.

"It's weird; even the air smells different now," he thought as he walked to the bus station, a mile away. He bought a one-way ticket to Coronado, California, and never looked back.

By the time Chris stepped off the bus in Coronado two days later, the reality of his decision hit him like a sledgehammer. The air carried the sharp scent of the Pacific mixed with the oil-stained asphalt of the naval base. The sun glared off the pavement like it was testing his endurance before the real trials began. He was really there, and there was no turning back. Chris had enlisted in the Navy with his sights set on the SEAL program. Saying the words and signing the papers had been easy. Living them and surviving them was another thing entirely.

Chris knew the statistics of those who didn't make it. The dropout rate was incredible, and looking around at the hardened recruits who stood beside him, Chris wasn't sure if he belonged. But that didn't matter. He hadn't come this far to fail.

BUD/S was hell.

Not the kind of hell most people imagined, it was worse.

His body became a battlefield. Blisters turned into open wounds, muscles locked in endless rebellion, and hunger gnawed at him until he forgot what full even felt like. The instructors didn't care—not about his pain, his exhaustion, or the part of him that wanted to give up. They existed to break him, to push him past what he thought was possible. To see if he was worth reforging.

The cold was the worst.

He remembered the first time they told them to piss on themselves for warmth. At first, he thought they were joking. Then he spent hours in the frigid Pacific, his body shaking so violently he couldn't feel his limbs, and pride suddenly didn't matter anymore. He did it. And for a few fleeting moments, warmth spread through his wetsuit before the ocean stripped it away, like a cruel reminder that nothing lasted here. Not comfort, not relief, not even sanity.

He ran until his legs gave out. He swam until his lungs screamed for air. For days, he went on barely any sleep, his mind teetering on the edge of delirium. The pain never stopped, but neither did Jackson.

The Hammer and the Anvil

Chris first noticed Jackson in the early days of training. The man was built like a machine: compact muscle, sharp movements, a face carved from stone. He was an enigma, carrying the kind of presence that made even the most hardened recruits fall in line.

But Jackson wasn't just another hardass. He had a different kind of influence to him. His voice wasn't just loud; it carried purpose. He didn't just punish; he molded. Chris didn't understand that until the fight.

It happened after a brutal drill when exhaustion had turned into aggression. The guy next to him shoved him in the chow line, and before Chris could think, his fist was already connecting with the guy's jaw. Chris barely registered the hit to his ribs before the fight was over.

Without a word, Jackson tapped Chris and told him to follow him outside. The door slammed shut as they stepped out, and suddenly, it was just the two of them.

Jackson pinned Chris with a stare that could have shattered glass. Unshaken. Unforgiving.

"What the hell was that?" Jackson said in a chilling, calm voice. It was the kind of quiet that came before an explosion.

Chris, still catching his breath, wiped blood from his lip. "Fucking dude put his hands on me first."

Jackson tilted his head slightly. "And?"

Chris blinked. "And what? I just told you."

Jackson stepped closer, the air between them tightening.

"You think out in the field, in the middle of a mission, you get to throw a punch because someone pisses you off?"

Chris clenched his jaw.

Jackson scoffed. "You think this is about being tough? You think your fists mean a damn thing out there?" He shook his head. "You're emotional, immature and think you have a lot to prove. That's gonna get you killed."

Chris's pulse pounded in his ears, but he stayed quiet.

For a moment, Jackson just stared at him, measuring him. Then, his voice dropped lower, steadier.

"I don't say this often, so you better listen, once. You've got potential. More than most. But potential don't mean shit without discipline. Without respect. You learn that? You might actually be worth a damn."

Chris swallowed hard. The weight of those words hit something profound inside him, something raw and unfamiliar.

Jackson walked back inside and left Chris alone as he thought about the meaning of the words.

No one had ever spoken to him like that. Not like an authority figure, not like an enemy, but he spoke to him like a man shaping steel over fire.

It was like a father speaking to a son.

That moment—that single conversation—became the anchor that kept Chris from quitting.

Whenever he thought about walking away, when the exhaustion and pain became too much, he heard Jackson's voice. 'Discipline. Respect. You might actually be worth a damn.'

Every time he thought about quitting, Jackson's faith made him stay.

When he finally made it through BUD/S, bruised, battered, and barely standing, Jackson was there, watching. Not smiling. Not clapping. Just nodding. He was like a blacksmith inspecting his work.

Chris had been broken, beaten, and pushed to the edge. He had been forged in fire, and for the first time in his life, he was stronger for it.

Finally, for the first time, Chris realized he had a person who believed in him.

Chapter 6

"Ohh, my god, yes!" April's shrill voice brought Chris out of the past. "Damn baby, that feels so good," she said while looking back at him.

Chris could feel his climax begin to rise. April screamed with pleasure as she shuddered and fell to the bed. Chris leaned down to kiss her neck, then he continued to thrust in and out of her from behind. April pressed her face into the pillow, moaning in ecstasy from feeling his stiff cock filling her. Chris continued to kiss April's neck and move with intense passion until he felt the pressure to explode inside of her. With a grunt, he released his juices into her.

"Ugh, yes!" he groaned.

Chris kneeled above April, sweaty. He leaned back for a few seconds, then rolled to his side. They were quiet for a few minutes, breathing heavily and enjoying the moment. He was about to tell her he had an early day and that she could leave when she cleaned up. But before he said anything, he heard April snoring.

Fuck, I ought to wake her up and tell her to leave, but I don't want to be a dick. I don't feel like this couple bullshit, though. Should I do it? Chris thought.

April wasn't the woman he wanted tonight. It was Amanda. She had begun to invade his dreams, slipping into his thoughts when he least expected it. Her soft laughter would echo through his mind, and her blue eyes would look at him with something dangerously close to adoration. It wasn't just lust; it was something more profound. It was something that unsettled him in the best possible way.

The first time Chris met Amanda, she had been just a kid. A cute kid, sure, but nothing more than that. A young teenager with wild energy and a smile that could make a room feel ten degrees brighter. Back then, she had been all arms and legs, still figuring out how to move in her skin. Chris was acutely aware of her schoolgirl crush on him; he just never took it seriously.

At first, her attempts to impress him had been adorably tragic.

Once, she sat down next to him, clearing her throat dramatically before dropping her voice into something she probably thought sounded sultry, but it came out awkward and forced.

"So, Chris, what are your thoughts on... stocks?"

Chris had barely managed to keep a straight face. He took a slow sip of his drink, playing along. "Stocks?"

Amanda nodded, her expression one of forced concentration. "Yeah. You know. Investing. The economy and... uhh, Wall Street stuff." She waved a hand as if that explained everything.

Chris leaned back in his chair, fighting back laughter. "Ohh yeah? You investing in anything specific?"

Amanda's brows scrunched together in obvious panic. "Uhm... Apple?"

Chris smirked. "Nice. Solid choice."

She visibly relaxed, as if she had just aced a test, and continued nodding, all serious. "Yeah, yeah, I think it's, umm, a really good time to buy. Because of, you know..." She faltered. "The... stock prices."

Chris had to press his lips together to keep from laughing. "This kid is hilarious," he thought.

She didn't give up, though. She tried to insert herself into his world by bringing up sports she had never watched, bands she clearly didn't listen to, and even military tactics, which resulted in one of the worst, most hilariously inaccurate explanations of Navy SEALs he'd ever heard.

But it was cute and funny. Back then, she was just a kid with a harmless crush, and he had been nothing more than a patient spectator, amused by her attempts to act older than she was.

Now, years later, she wasn't a kid anymore.

And she was no longer just someone to humor.

She was the woman he wanted. The woman who had begun to haunt his nights.

Along the way, he noticed how beautiful she was as a woman. Around her twentieth birthday, he noticed her shorts becoming tighter and shorter. They were molding to her beautiful tight ass. Her breasts defied gravity and always teased him through her shirts. He spent many nights thinking about her. However, his devotion to his friendship with Jackson meant he could never act on his feelings. Plus, he figured he was way too old for her anyway.

* * * * *

"So...he called you a slut, huh? Well, that means that he really likes you," Lori said as she wiped the nail polish off her toes.

"What? Why would you say that?" Amanda frowned.

"Because, duh, he was jealous."

Amanda thought about what she said, chewing on her lip and thinking it over. "Uhm, well...maybe he was. I mean, he was glued to me when I first saw him. He didn't even introduce that girl. Plus, sometimes I catch him staring at my ass when he's at the house, then he turns away real quick. But I see him."

Lorie smirked. "You just love teasing him and watching him squirm, don't ya?"

Amanda grinned. "Yeah. You know one night when my dad ran to the grocery store for some more meat, I went in the living room and sat on the floor right in front of BT."

"Trying to tease him a little bit?" Lori asked, still focused on her toes.

"Mmhmm. I laid down after a few minutes with my ass in the air. I had on that small bikini top and those small white terry cloth shorts."

"Ohh yeah, I remember those. They're kind of thin right?" asked Lori.

"Yeah. So sexy. I started to spread my legs my legs a little bit too. Then during a commercial I started to stretch right there. Ass in the air and everything." Amanda said with a laugh.

"Face down, ass up!" Lori laughed.

Amanda grinned, but her thoughts drifted back. "I have good memories about flirting with him. I just don't know. I mean maybe he was jealous, but...still. You know what I mean?"

"Hmm." Lori wiped the last bit of polish off.

"One time when I was around eighteen, BT was in the backyard helping my dad build the deck. Well, dad left to go get more of... something for it, and he went to lie down in the shade under a tree. I was upstairs watching him, chest out, sweat dripping, muscles poppin' everywhere. And he was wearing a pair of fitted pants. He had me felling hot! I just wanted to go lick him."

"Uhh...okay, I guess." Lori made a face. "But licking sweat is nasty."

Amanda rolled her eyes. "Anyway! So, I walked down to the backyard and stood over to him. He had his eyes closed, and I didn't wanna startle him. So, I just stood there, staring at his face."

"You mean like a creepy stalker?"

"No, not like that. Well, I mean yeah I guess it was creepy. But at the time I thought it was sexy. His brown skin, beautiful face, and sexy lips. I just wanted those lips between my legs."

Lori let out a laugh. "So, what did you do?"

Amanda smirked. "I leaned down and kissed him. He didn't move at first, so I, uhh... might've licked his chest too." She giggled. "And then when I looked up, his eyes were wide open, just staring at me. I panicked and ran back inside."

"What! Did he follow you?"

Amanda nodded. "Yep. I got to my room and shut the door. I was so fucking embarrassed, and I just knew he was going to tell my dad. I looked out the window and couldn't see him right... then I hear footsteps coming up the stairs. I was like, is this it? Are we about to fuck?"

Lori's eyes widened. "What happened? I've never heard this shit."

"He stopped outside my room. I could hear him breathing. He knocked on the door and said, 'We need to talk', or some shit. I don't even remember, I was too busy freaking out. So, I took my clothes off and went to the door, but then my fucking dad came home and called his name. He went back outside, and we never talked about it."

"Noooo! Girl, you are wild. Licking your dad's friend in the damn yard." Lori cracked up.

Amanda laughed. "Yeah, I definitely used my dildo that day. Whew, it was wet in there."

Lori fake gagged. "Girl, please."

Amanda sighed. "Ugh, I don't know if he's jealous. Life's a bitch, right? He brought that chick to my party, so he can't care that much. You'd think a thirty-year-old man would be smart enough not to bring a woman when he knows I like him.

Lori got up to grab a drink. "Yeah, you'd hope, but sometimes men are stupid."

Amanda licked her lips. "Mmm, I just wanna rub on that bald head while he works my damn body."

"Well, he obviously noticed the dress if he reacted like that. If I were you, I'd try it again, alone, and see if he has the same reaction."

"Yeah, this is a sexy ass dress. Maybe I should try it at his house. I just wish I knew if that chick will be there," Amanda said as she hopped up, slipping on her shoes and fixing her makeup.

Lori asked slowly, curiously, "Where are you going?"

Amanda met her gaze in the mirror, voice firm. "To make BT fuck me or tell me he's not into me."

She grabbed her bag and walked out.

Lori shook her head and poured another drink.

Chapter 7

Amanda knew the walk to Chris's house would be long, but she didn't care. Her car was in the shop, she didn't want to leave Lori stranded, and she definitely wasn't about to explain this mission to her dad. Nothing was stopping her tonight.

The night air was crisp against her skin as she tugged her cropped jacket tighter around her body. Good for style, bad for warmth. Switching from heels to her NOBULL runners had been a smart move; her feet would've never survived the hike otherwise.

Streetlights stretched along each block, casting pools of soft yellow glow on the pavement, enough to make her feel safe. But every so often, the overhanging trees swallowed the light, throwing shadows across her path. The winding road forced the sidewalk to end abruptly on one side and reappear on the other, making her dart across the street at annoying intervals. Another small frustration, but nothing that would deter her.

The cold wind bit at her legs and kissed her cheeks, turning them pink. But there was something about the air tonight, it wasn't just sharp and unforgiving. The scent of trees and fresh grass softened its edge, making it feel less hostile.

In the darker stretches, she glanced up and found the moon; bright, full, hanging low like it was watching her.

Amanda wasn't turning back. Not now.

Finally, she reached his house. The wide sprawling farmhouse style front porch was accented with bluish-grey and large pops of red, that gave way to the bright red front door. The landscape was immaculate, and the sidewalk lights provided just the right amount of light. His car was parked outside, but she didn't recognize the other car to the left. Amanda stopped for a few minutes in the yard to catch her breath and relax from the walk. As she ascended the steps of the porch, a wave of nervous energy engulfed her mind. It was about this mission.

Finally, Amanda got to Chris's house. She spotted his car, then another one to the left, April's car. Her stomach clenched, but her feet kept moving.

Ohh well, I'm still going for it. Then, doubt began to creep into her mind. What if he tells my dad? Will this make things too awkward for everyone? I need to follow my heart on this. Or... maybe my pussy. The thought made her chuckle under her breath, but it didn't stop the swirl of nerves climbing up her spine.

Then another thought slammed into her. What if April tries to fight me? Amanda rolled her shoulders. I can take her, easy. But is BT even worth it? She hesitated mid-step. What if this all blows up? What happens to him and dad if it does? The friendship between them, would it survive? I would be the reason it cracked.

Her thoughts spun in circles. And then, she forced them down. I don't know. But this is it.

She lifted her hand to ring the doorbell.

But, before she could touch it, the door swung open.

Chris stood there, shirtless, wearing only unbuttoned dark jeans and retro Jordan 3s. A cigar rested between his lips, unlit, and his clenched fists made it clear he had been ready to fight whoever was on the other side of the door.

Amanda froze.

His sharp brown eyes locked onto hers, scanning her from head to toe. A wave of heat coiled through her, but she shoved it down.

This isn't how I pictured this, she thought.

Chris's face stayed unreadable, and his body was tense like a live wire.

"Umm... wh...what are you doing here?" His voice was low, firm.

Amanda opened her mouth, "I...I...umm." Nothing else came out.

She couldn't speak. The way he talked to her earlier, the humiliation, the frustration, and the sting of rejection, it all rushed back in a tidal wave.

Her excitement? Gone.

Before she could find her voice, a second one cut through the moment like a blade.

"What is she doing here?" April shrieked.

Amanda didn't need to turn her head. She knew whose voice that was.

April stood in the doorway now, wrapped in Chris's white polo, a thong, hair wild, makeup half-smudged, and still smelling like sweet beach.

Chris didn't acknowledge her. Neither did Amanda.

The silence stretched on, seemingly for forever.

Finally, Amanda swallowed down the lump in her throat. "I'm sorry. I'm leaving right now. I feel so stupid."

She turned to leave, but her legs felt heavy, her face hot with embarrassment. The sharp sting behind her eyes warned her tears were coming. Hell no. Not here. Not in front of them.

Then, suddenly, she wasn't on the ground anymore. Chris's strong arm locked around her waist, lifting her like she weighed nothing.

"What the hell?"

Before she could finish her protest, he carried her inside and dumped her onto the couch. Her body bounced from the force of it, a small gasp escaping her lips. The landing wasn't graceful, it was jarring, and disorienting.

Amanda sat up, breath shallow. "What the fuck was that?"

Chris didn't respond; he just shot her a look that shut her up immediately.

With her mouth closed, the tension in the room thickened.

"What the hell is going on with you two?" April screeched.

Chris turned his head toward her, expression unreadable, jaw tight. Then, without a word, he walked down the hall.

Amanda and April watched him in stunned silence. Minutes passed, then he reappeared with April's clothes and her handbag. Chris shoved them toward her. April stood there, staring at him in disbelief, tears welling in her eyes.

Chris pinched the bridge of his nose, exhaling slowly before speaking. His voice was calm, but ice cold.

"April, I need you to leave. Now."

She stared at him, lips trembling.

Chris sighed, his tone softening just slightly. "I'll call you tomorrow, but I need you to go. Please."

April's silence cut deeper than words. She held his gaze, pain flashing behind her wet lashes. Then, in one last act of defiance, she peeled his polo off, letting it drop to the floor. She stood there, bare-chested, vulnerable, watching him.

Amanda looked away, but Chris didn't. His expression never changed. Foot tapping. Arms crossed. Waiting. April held his stare, chest rising and falling. Then, without a word, she pulled on her tight dress, grabbed her bag, and threw them both one last glare before stomping out and slamming the door behind her.

The moment stretched in silence.

Amanda's chest rose and fell, her mind still spinning from what just happened. Chris finally turned his head, his deep brown eyes locking onto hers. Amanda's breath caught.

For a moment, she was glad April was gone. That was until Chris turned around and looked at her. Then her nerves started to come back.

He turned his back to her and put his hands on his head. He did a silent count to ten so he could calm down. As he finished his silent count, he turned back around to face her. His eyes were calmer than before, but she could still tell he was pissed.

"What are you doing here, Amanda?" he asked calmly.

"Well, I really wanted to see you," Amanda said quietly.

"You really wanted to see me," he repeated. "Okay, well you saw me; now you can go home. It's late. So, I'll drive behind you to make sure you get there okay. I won't say anything to LT about this." He said while searching for his keys.

"That won't work. I didn't drive."

He looked up at her, noticing her pinkish face and legs; then he walked over to the window to confirm her story.

"The hell, who dropped you off then? I didn't hear you."

"No one. I walked."

Chris stood there staring at her for what felt like never ending time. She could see his face changing, filling with frustration.

"You walked from your house to my house in those clothes?" he asked dubiously, through clenched teeth. Amanda was nervous to say yes, so she nodded her head in the affirmative.

"You mean to tell me you walked all the way here wearing that? Alone and at night? What the fuck is wrong with you? Damnit Amanda!" he said yelling at this point.

But Amanda was not about to let him yell at her, no matter how nervous she was. Not this night. Tonight was about what she wanted. She stood up and got in his face.

"Who the hell you think you talking to? No one yells at me like that. Even my dad doesn't yell at me like that. You need to calm your ass down!" she yelled back at him. Raising her voice to match his level. "I don't have to answer to you. You're not my father."

"I'm not saying that I am Amanda, I was just worried something could have happened to you. You don't see how crazy this is?"

"The only thing crazy is that you keep pretending that you aren't attracted to me. You know I like you. I want you right now. I've wanted you for years. Fucking years, Okay?"

Chris didn't respond, he just stood there with a confused look on his face. He pursed his lips as to start speaking, but nothing came out. The words Amanda spoke echoed in his mind. He knew she had a crush on him, enjoyed flirting with him, and teasing him. But, never in his mind did he think she had a burning desire for him. The years of seeing her in revealing outfits, her flirting, her intense looks that she would give him, they all made sense to him now. With a minute of silence between them gone, after Chris's rambling thoughts subsided, he finally spoke.

"I, uhh, I feel like this is too big of a conversation for us to have tonight. Especially since, well, you're LT's daughter for fucks sake. I mean I can't even count the ways having sex with you would fuck up my life. Hell, our lives." Chris said with a worried chuckle.

"Would you please stop bringing my father into this. This is my life. Yes, he and my mom gave me life, but they should be happy if I'm living it in a way that brings me happiness. I don't know if things would work out or get serious with us, but I want to find out." Amanda said in a calmer tone while lightly grabbing his left arm. "I mean shouldn't we at least try?"

Chris exhaled. "I do find you attractive, yes. And I must admit, recently I've been thinking about you in...not so much of a platonic sense. Listen, I really think—" was all Chris could get out before Amanda made her move.

Chris was mid-sentence when Amanda reached for his hand. Her touch trembled slightly as she guided it up to her right breast, pressed him against the soft curve through her thin top. His voice faltered, breath catching. The look in her eyes begged him to stay with her in the moment, uncertain, aching, needing.

She slid closer, her body was now brushing against his. She took his other hand and placed it firmly on her waist. Her heart thundered in her chest as she tilted her face toward his, lips parted, unsure if he would meet her halfway. Chris hesitated for a second—just one—before lowering his head.

Their lips met, slow at first, then deeper. The kiss was messy, charged, and hungry with the kind of heat that came from waiting too long. Their mouths opened wider, tongues mingling, desperate for more. Her hands roamed over his chest, sliding down his sides, then lower. Her fingertips brushed along the waistband of his pants like a question she was afraid to ask out loud.

She found him already hard beneath his jeans, and her fingers lingered, tracing the shape of him through the fabric. He gasped softly, his hips involuntarily pressing into her palm. Amanda's hand trembled as she cupped him more firmly, heat flooding between her thighs. She wasn't thinking about what she was doing, just following her burning desire to have him and feel everything.

Chris buried his face in her neck, breathing her in, one hand tightening on her waist while the other slid over her breast. There was no finesse to their dance, just raw, eager touches from two people standing on the edge of something wild and new.

Chris's breathing grew heavier as Amanda's body pressed into his. His hands slid up her thighs and under the hem of her dress, fingers finally settling on the curve of her ass. She gasped softly at his touch, her body instinctively grinding into him, both of them caught in the messy rhythm of need and uncertainty. Their mouths found each other again, desperate kisses, lips, and teeth clashing as their hands wandered.

They stumbled together onto the couch, breathless. Chris landed on his back, and Amanda straddled him, her dress hiked up around her hips. Her hands trembled slightly as she reached for his jeans, fumbling with the button, then the zipper, fingers clumsy with anticipation. She finally tugged them down, inch by inch, until his cock sprang free: thick, flushed, and already leaking.

A wave of heat pulsed between her legs at the sight of him. His cologne still clung faintly to his skin, especially at his waist, and as she leaned in, the earthy, masculine, intoxicating scent flooded her senses. Her mouth watered. Body ached. She wrapped her fingers around his girth, and the weight of him in her hand made her heart race harder.

She looked up, her voice low and a little breathless. "Do you want me to put it in my mouth?"

Chris swallowed hard, his pupils blown wide with desire. "Yes... Please. Put it in that warm, smart mouth of yours."

That made her smile. A crooked, nervous grin, half confident, half unsure, but all desire.

She lowered her head, her lips brushing the head of his cock, then slowly enveloping him. The heat of her mouth made Chris buck slightly beneath her, a choked groan spilling from his throat.

"Ohh my God," he moaned, his voice strained and shaky. "What the... what the—"

His words dissolved into low, continuous moans as her mouth worked him. She used slow, tentative strokes at first, guided more by instinct than experience. Amanda moved carefully, testing how much of him she could take in her mouth, listening to every breath, every reaction, adjusting with each flick of her tongue.

Amanda's lips wrapped around his cock with hungry, wet devotion, her tongue swirling and teasing, lost in the moment. Chris couldn't take it any longer as his breath ragged, his thighs tensed, and every nerve in his body lit up. He sat up abruptly, hands moving to her dress, tugging at the tight fabric like he needed her bare skin more than air.

She pulled back, lips slick, and raised her arms to help him strip her down. As he worked the dress over her curves, she slipped off her panties and tossed them aside, the air thick with anticipation.

Chris gave her a firm smack on the ass, more instinct than plan, and the moan Amanda let out was part surprise, part invitation. He stood up, picked her up with shaky confidence, and lowered her onto the couch, spreading her legs and hooking them over his shoulders.

Without a word, he buried his face between her thighs.

Amanda gasped, then whimpered as his tongue found her clit. He licked and sucked in steady, eager strokes while sliding a finger deep inside her, curling just enough to make her hips buck. She cried out, clutching the back of his head, grinding against his mouth like her life depended on it. Her thighs tightened around him, and he welcomed it, letting her trap him there as he devoured her with an intensity that bordered on worship.

Then, finally, he pulled back, his lips wet with her. He looked up, voice rough. "Do you want me inside you?"

"Yes. Put it in me now!" Her answer came without hesitation, her voice shaking with need.

"Okay...let me grab a condom."

"No," Amanda breathed, eyes still closed, her hand reaching out to catch his arm before he could move. "You don't need that with me. Please...I want to feel all of you."

Her words hit him like a spark to dry kindling. Any thoughts of consequence disappeared.

"Okay," he said, barely a whisper, already pulling her close again.

He knelt on the couch, guiding himself to her entrance. Amanda held her breath as he pushed inside: slow, steady, stretching her open inch by inch. She gasped, clutching at his sides as the thick weight of his cock filled her. The warmth of her pussy wrapped around him, slick and hot, making them both moan into each other's mouths.

He started to move with slow thrusts that built with every heartbeat. Her legs lifted onto his shoulders, and he rocked into her, faster now, chasing the edge of something they weren't sure they were ready for.

And then—he stopped.

Just...stopped.

Chris pulled out, breathing hard, sweat clinging to his chest, and sat back on his legs, staring at her.

Amanda blinked, stunned.

"What the fuck? Why did you stop? Did you cum already?" she asked, still flushed, her skin pink and glowing from the pleasure. "It's okay if you did. We can just take a break."

Chris shook his head, guilt already creeping into his features.

"I just...I don't think we can do this. Not like this."

Amanda sat up, confused and hurt. "What? You don't like me or something? Is that it?"

"No. That's not it at all," he said quickly, running a hand over his head. "I like you too much. That's the problem. I don't want this to be just a hookup. Not after everything we've been through. Not while we're in the middle of fighting."

Her face softened, but her eyes were glassy, voice trembling. "So, what now? You just stop? Walk away like it didn't happen?"

He sighed. "No, I just need...time. I don't want to screw this up. I don't want you to feel used."

Amanda looked down, her throat tightening. "Okay. I guess. But what does this mean?"

"It means..." He trailed off, then stepped away, grabbing his pants. "I don't know yet. Just...please get dressed and wait for me in the car."

She stood silently, nodding. "Okay...okay."

Chris handed her the keys and disappeared down the hallway. Amanda pulled her dress back on, her limbs still humming from everything that just happened, even as her chest ached with questions.

She opened the door, walked out, and closed it softly behind her.

Chapter 8

The ride back to Amanda's house was thick with silence, the kind that buzzed just beneath the skin. Chris had his music app on shuffle, letting a chaotic mix of genres fill the heavy space between them. Every few songs, he would skip anything too emotional, too pointed, his fingers fidgeting on the steering wheel. But no amount of background noise could drown out what hung between them.

Amanda stared out the window, her forehead resting against the cool glass. She hadn't said a word, hadn't even looked at Chris since they left. He tried not to glance at her and keep his eyes glued to the road, but every few seconds, they drifted to the way her short dress had crept up her thighs, to the subtle, frustrated tension in how she crossed her legs.

Just one peek, that should be harmless, Chris told himself.

He let his gaze slide over her bare skin—smooth, pristine, impossible to ignore. But when he looked back up, Amanda was staring right at him. The anger, confusion, and hurt on her face made his stomach twist. He smiled sheepishly, hoping to defuse the moment, but she didn't return it. She just turned back to the window, a silent wall between them.

The endless string of traffic lights stretched the drive into an eternity.

Chris cleared his throat. "Wow, these lights are taking forever tonight, huh?"

"Uh-huh," Amanda mumbled, her tone flat, distant.

The tightness in Chris's chest grew unbearable. He gripped the steering wheel tighter, searching for the right words, any words that could bridge the gap.

"Amanda, listen to me," he said finally. "I like you. A lot. And... I'm not sorry about what happened tonight. I just, I want to do this the smart way."

Amanda turned her head slightly, her voice sharp. "And what exactly is the smart way, BT?"

He sighed, the weight of her question sitting heavy in his chest. "I don't know exactly. But arguing and fucking on my couch, isn't it. I want it to mean something. I want you to mean something."

Her laugh was bitter, wounded. "You have to think about risk. I just want you. I don't care what anyone else thinks. I'm not a little girl."

Chris opened his mouth to respond but froze when he caught her movement. Amanda's hand was sliding up the hem of her dress, exposing more of those dangerous thighs. His heart hammered against his ribs.

"What are you doing?" he hissed, voice tight. "We're almost at your house. Put your dress down."

The light turned green, and Chris forced his eyes back to the road, but not before catching the sly, daring glint in Amanda's eye.

He chuckled, shaking his head at how much she infuriated him and how badly he still wanted her. Amanda watched him, confused, the edges of her anger softening just a little.

Chris mouthed along to the country song playing on the radio, pretending to focus, pretending he wasn't completely undone by her.

Amanda's voice broke through the music, soft but piercing. "Do you really want me?"

He swallowed hard. "Of course I do. Yes. But it's not that simple."

"Why not?" she pressed, her voice smaller now, almost pleading.

Chris's hands tightened on the wheel. "Cause... LT's like a father to me. If he ever found out about us, it would crush him. I can't just pretend that don't matter. I can't betray him like that."

Amanda sat back in her seat, the fight draining out of her as the weight of his words settled in. She turned to look out the window again, her reflection blurred against the glass.

And for the rest of the drive, they let the silence say everything they couldn't.

When they reached Amanda's house, Chris had barely put the Jeep into park before she yanked the door open and jumped out. She slammed the door, which echoed like a gunshot in the heavy night air. She moved stiffly up the walkway, her arms wrapped tightly around herself. The porch light above the door buzzed softly, casting a yellow glow over everything, making the scene feel even more surreal.

Halfway to the steps, Amanda slowed. She spotted Jackson sitting on the top step, hunched over his phone. His face was illuminated by the blue screen, highlighting the tired lines etched deep around his eyes and mouth. Amanda's shoulders tensed like she was bracing for a confrontation she didn't have the strength to fight.

But Jackson just looked up at her, really looked, and must have seen everything written across her face: the anger, the confusion, the heartbreak. He didn't say a word. No lectures, no questions. He simply nodded once, slowly, and turned his gaze back to his phone as she passed him by.

Chris sat frozen in the Jeep for a moment, gripping the steering wheel so tightly his knuckles started to ache. His heart pounded against his ribs, the adrenaline still crackling under his skin. Finally, he scrubbed a hand over his face, let out a low groan, and climbed out of the Jeep.

The night air was thick with humidity, and the faint scent of cut grass and hot asphalt lingered in the background. Chris shoved his hands into his pockets as he walked toward the steps, trying to compose himself. As he got closer, he caught the look on Jackson's face—a weak smile, heavy with exhaustion, like he'd been carrying the weight of the world for far too long.

"Hey, LT. Long night?" Chris offered his voice strained but casual.

Jackson chuckled dryly without looking up. "Yup. Very long." His thumb absently scrolled across his screen before he finally tucked the phone away. "So... where'd you find her?"

Chris shifted his weight from foot to foot, suddenly feeling like a teenager again, caught sneaking in late. "Well... umm... she kind of walked to my house," he said, scratching the back of his neck. "I didn't know she was coming. I was just home with April when she showed up."

He didn't have to explain more. The unspoken history hung between them—Amanda's crush on him had been obvious for a while. Still, it had always been treated like a harmless joke. Something easy to dismiss. Not anymore.

Jackson grunted softly, his brow furrowing. "Hmm. She okay? She looked pretty upset."

Chris nodded quickly. "Yeah. She's fine. Just... tired, I think."

Jackson took a long breath, his shoulders sagging under an invisible weight. He stared out into the yard, the grass glistening faintly under the porch light. Chris sensed the conversation was ending and took a step backward, ready to leave, until Jackson's voice stopped him.

"It's just that..." Jackson said, his words slow and heavy, like pulling stones from his chest. "She's an adult now. But I still feel like I gotta protect her. I just... don't know how to anymore." His voice cracked slightly at the end.

Chris stayed where he was, leaning back against the porch railing, giving the man space to speak.

Jackson ran a hand over his face, visibly struggling. "She's got so much of her mother in her," he said finally. "That fire, that stubbornness. And that spirit... God, she could light up a room just by walking into it. Just like Dara."

He paused, swallowing hard.

"I wanted Amanda to be different. To have that light, but without the darkness that came with it." His voice grew quieter, rougher. "Dara always wanted more—more money, more attention, more everything. I thought if I loved her hard enough, I could fill the gaps. That she'd stay. But love... love alone can't carry two people forever."

Chris felt his chest tighten. He hadn't known this side of Jackson, hadn't seen the old scars still bleeding under the surface.

"When she ran off with that piece of shit..." Jackson's jaw tightened. "I wanted to kill 'em both. Her, for leaving us. Him, just because he existed. Fuck that guy. Last I heard, he got her hooked-on drugs. Sweet Dara, the girl I met in high school, turned into someone I didn't even recognize."

He shook his head, staring down at the cracked concrete below the steps. "I look at Amanda and I see her. I see everything I loved—and everything that broke me. And I'm terrified. Terrified that one day Amanda's gonna wake up, decide her old man ain't good enough, and disappear too."

The silence stretched between them, heavy with pain and things neither of them knew how to fix.

Chris gazed out at the dark street; the stars blurred behind a thin veil of clouds. He thought about Amanda upstairs—so strong, stubborn, and heartbreakingly vulnerable underneath it all. And he thought about what happened tonight. What might happen again if he wasn't careful.

"I'm sorry, Chris. It's late. You should head home," Jackson finally said, pushing to his feet, his movements slow with exhaustion. "Thanks for looking out for her."

Chris stood, too, forcing a reassuring smile. "It's not a problem, sir. I'm just glad she's back safe."

He made it halfway to the Jeep before a grin tugged at his lips. He turned, calling back over his shoulder.

"Ohh, hey, LT!"

Jackson glanced up.

Chris smirked. "Please find that dress she wore tonight. And burn it."

For a beat, Jackson just stared at him. Then he let out a deep, rumbling laugh—the first real laugh Chris had heard from him in a long time.

"With pleasure," Jackson said, the ghost of a smile lingering on his face as he disappeared inside.

Chris climbed into the Jeep, chuckling quietly to himself. But as he pulled away from the curb, a nagging thought whispered through his mind.

Some things, once lit, don't burn out so easily.

Chapter 9

Lori was already asleep when Amanda burst through the bedroom door. She stripped off the dress in one frantic motion, tossing it aside like it physically hurt to wear it. Grabbing a thin T-shirt from the chair in the corner, she pulled it over her head, slid into a pair of white cotton shorts, and crawled under the covers with desperate speed.

Lori stirred, blinking blearily at her. She opened her mouth to ask what was wrong, but a sharp knock echoed from the hallway before she could get a word out.

"We're sleeping, Dad!" Amanda yelled toward the closed door, her voice cracking slightly.

A pause.

"You just got here. Let Lori sleep. Come to the study, we need to talk," her father's voice replied, calm but firm.

Amanda flopped onto her back and let out a low groan. Shit.

This night was officially the worst. All she wanted was to crawl under the covers, block out reality, and pretend everything had gone differently.

Sighing heavily, she threw off the blanket, yanked open a drawer, and tugged on a fresh pair of longer shorts. Her movements were sharp and angry. She stomped to the door and pulled it open.

Her father stood there, leaning casually against the doorframe, a tight, unreadable smile on his face. Without a word, they walked toward the study, their footsteps muffled by the thick rug. Amanda kept her arms folded tightly across her chest the whole way, feeling cornered and exposed.

Inside the study, Jackson sank into his big leather chair, stretching back with a long, weary breath. He laced his fingers behind his head, staring up at the ceiling for a moment before lowering his gaze to her.

Amanda stood stubbornly in the middle of the room, hands on her hips, glaring at him.

She couldn't stop the small, ironic smile tugging at her lips.

"Chris does the same thing," she thought, remembering how he would tilt his head back and breathe deep whenever he was trying not to lose it with her.

Finally, Jackson straightened and spoke, cutting right to the chase.

"Amanda... what's going on?"

Amanda shrugged, her smile vanishing.

"That's not an answer," he said, drumming his fingers lightly against the desk, an old nervous habit she recognized from childhood.

She could see it—the way he was fighting himself, the way he was trying to stay calm, careful, bracing for whatever truth might come flying at him. He had always hated these kinds of talks. Amanda flashed back to the painfully awkward "sex talk" when she was thirteen, the PowerPoint presentation, the dolls, and the painfully detailed videos he made her watch about birth. She had been mortified then... and somehow, it felt even worse now.

"Is it me?" Jackson finally asked, his voice softer. "Am I not a good father?"

"No, Dad. No, it's not you," Amanda said, her arms falling to her sides. Her voice cracked with the effort to sound steady.

"You seem restless. Irritated all the time," Jackson continued, tapping his fingers restlessly. "I don't always say anything, but I notice. I notice everything. You're my kid. Doesn't matter how old you get. I'll always worry."

Amanda looked away, blinking hard. She didn't want to do this right now. She didn't want to lay herself bare. She was too tired, confused, and raw from the rollercoaster of emotions she had already endured tonight.

"It's just us, kiddo," Jackson said, his voice dropping to something closer to a plea. "We're all each other has. I need you to talk to me. Tell me what's going on in that pretty head of yours."

She stayed silent, staring down at the floor. Her chest felt too tight to speak.

Jackson sighed, louder this time, like he was trying to blow away the tension.

"Is this about Chris?"

The sound of his name hit her like a slap. Amanda jerked her gaze to the floor, her cheeks flaming. Her whole chest turned red, betraying her even if her lips didn't move.

Jackson's face twisted in a mix of understanding and dread.

"Look, I get it. You're both adults," he said carefully. "But he's been around for years. Like... an older brother to you, you know."

Amanda snorted a rough, bitter sound. "You don't know anything," she snapped.

"Then tell me. Please."

But Amanda shook her head. Her whole body screamed exhaustion.

"I'm tired. Can I just go to bed?" she said, staring him dead in the eye.

Jackson looked at her for a long moment. The lines around his mouth deepened.

"Yeah. Sure, kiddo. Sleep well."

Amanda turned on her heel and stomped out of the room, her heart pounding in her ears.

Jackson watched her go, his body sinking deeper into the chair. A strange, heavy sensation bloomed in his chest; a tightness, a sharp pain radiating down his arm. He tried to push himself up from the desk, but his legs buckled. His arms swept across the desk, sending himself paperweights and pens clattering to the floor with a loud crash.

Amanda, halfway down the hall, whipped around at the sound.

"Daddy!" she screamed, sprinting back into the study.

She found him slumped beside the desk, his face pale and drawn.

"It's okay, honey," he rasped, barely above a whisper. "But I need you to call 911."

Amanda's fingers trembled as she bolted back to her room. She fumbled for her phone, her sobs ripping from her throat. Lori sat up groggily, blinking in confusion.

"What's wrong?" Lori asked, her voice thick with sleep.

"It's Daddy, something's wrong!" Amanda gasped, before pressing the phone to her ear.

"Emergency services, what's the nature of your emergency?" the calm operator's voice cut through the chaos.

"My dad, he's on the floor! He told me to call! I don't know what's wrong and I'm freaking the fuck out!" Amanda cried into the receiver.

"It's okay, ma'am. Is the address registered with your mobile phone your location?"

"What? I mean yeah, it's the same place."

"Okay, I have help already on the way. I'm going to stay with you, but I need you to do something for me, okay? Stay calm. Talk to him. Keep him awake."

Amanda nodded yes frantically, even though the operator couldn't see her. She clutched the phone tighter and ran back toward the study, her heart hammering against her ribs.

* * * * *

Amanda held her phone, and with shaking fingers, she called Chris. The hospital lights formed a harsh glare around her as she recorded the voicemail.

"Chris, something happened to Daddy. Please come meet us at the hospital," she sobbed, barely getting the words out before ending the call.

Chris was the only person she could think of.

The only one who had ever made the storm inside her slow down enough to breathe.

Awkward or not, angry or not, she needed him.

At the hospital, Chris paced the long corridors like a man who couldn't find his footing. The floors creaked softly under his boots, their fake wood pattern worn from too many restless nights and worried families.

The sharp change from the warm hallway to the sterile waiting area, blue and red triangle-patterned carpet, and stiff pleather benches felt jarring. The artwork on the walls tried too hard to be soothing: pastel beaches, watercolor fields of lavender, endless ocean horizons.

Chris forced himself to look at the paintings, to stay calm.

I grew up on beaches like that, he thought grimly. The place where I first became a man. Where I met LT. Where everything started.

His stomach twisted.

And now... what if it ends here?

Every few steps, his eyes betrayed him. They darted toward Amanda, who sat stiffly on a green pleather bench, her arms wrapped around herself. She kept stealing glances at him, too, but the moment their eyes met, she looked away, chewing her lower lip until it turned red.

Neither of them spoke to each other.

Amanda tapped her foot against the ugly carpet, feeling like she might crawl out of her skin. The sports show on the muted television blurred in her ears with commentators droning on about stats and possible trades, the world still spinning as hers was shattering.

Every time Chris passed her, her heart thumped, hoping he might sit beside her.

But he didn't.

He couldn't.

The wall between them was thick with anger, confusion, and guilt.

Chris hadn't even known about Jackson until he randomly checked his phone an hour earlier, intending to put on music.

He'd silenced it earlier, trying to shut the world out after the chaos of the night.

When he saw Amanda's voicemail, he almost ignored it out of reflex.

What the hell does she want now? he had thought.

But when he heard her tear-streaked voice... his blood ran cold. The aura of Amanda's words flowed past his emotions from the evening. All Chris heard was, "LT, ambulance, and hospital."

He didn't even think. He threw on some Jeans, a T-shirt and boots. He grabbed his keys and ran out the door.

He floored it the entire thirty-five-minute drive, dodging traffic and ignoring the speed limits.

And now he was here, pacing and helpless.

Goddammit, old man. You better be okay, he thought.

Chris's jaw clenched when he caught Amanda looking at him again. A part of him blamed her.

What if the stress of tonight pushed LT too far? What if it was our fault? Hell, it's her fault. She's the one that came to my house.

The thought made him sick.

Amanda must have sensed it, too. She shrank into herself, rubbing her hands up and down her bare arms as if warding off an invisible chill.

Third time today I've been pissed at her, Chris thought bitterly. That's gotta be a record.

Finally, the doors to the ER hallway swung open, and a doctor stepped out.

Amanda shot to her feet, and Chris walked closer.

The doctor, an older man with thinning gray hair and deep bags under his eyes, gave them a weary smile.

"Hello, I'm Dr. Frank," he said, tearing his mask off quickly. "We got some of the test results back. Mr. Branson suffered a mild heart attack. We've admitted him for observation overnight. He'll be going for a heart catheterization shortly."

Amanda swayed slightly, her face turning bright red as her hands flew to her mouth. Her eyes flooded instantly with tears she couldn't hold back. She was in shock and couldn't say a word to Dr. Frank.

Chris stepped forward, his voice steady, even though he felt like he was standing on broken glass.

"Sorry Doc, Amanda is just in shock about her dad. What exactly does the heart 'tapazation' involve, Doc?"

"Heart catheterization, yes." Dr. Frank nodded briskly. "So, what we do is insert a catheter through an artery, usually the radial artery in the wrist or the femoral artery in the groin. We guide it up to the heart, inject a contrast dye, and take images under X-ray to find blockages. If we find something serious, we'll try to fix it right then and there."

Chris nodded again, absorbing the information like a soldier taking orders.

"Okay, thank you for coming out and letting us know what's going on."

"Sure thing Mister..."

"Temple, but you can call me Chris. Been a friend of the family for a long time."

"Alright Chris, I will let y'all know when he's done with the procedure," Dr. Frank smiled gently and retreated through the doors.

Amanda could only nod mutely, her voice locked behind the lump in her throat. Chris blew a sigh of relief as he turned to Amanda, his body aching with helplessness.

"You doing okay, Amanda?" he asked, voice gentler than it had been all night.

Amanda shook her head, no, tears sliding silently down her face.

"I don't... I don't really know what to say or ask or anything. I just want him to be okay. Will you stay here with me, please?" Amanda asked in a high-pitched voice, trying to hold back the monsoon of tears.

Chris didn't even think twice.

"Yeah. I'll stay," he said, dragging a chair a few feet away from her bench to give them both some breathing room. "I'm not leaving you here alone."

Amanda gave him a tiny, grateful smile before staring down at the ugly carpet again.

Chris sat back, forcing himself to breathe evenly. To wait. To hope.

"Hey, where's your friend, Lori?" he asked after a few minutes of heavy silence.

"She left," Amanda muttered. "Lori is a great friend, but neither of us is equipped to deal with this kind of shit. She panics sometimes, and she'd just freak me out worse."

Chris snorted softly. "Then her leaving was a smart move."

They sat in uneasy silence, watching highlights from some basketball game on the muted TV.

Another hour passed.

Finally, Dr. Frank returned, folded papers in hand, a little more spring in his step.

"Chris, Amanda," he said warmly. "The heart cath went well. Mr. Branson had two blockages, but we placed stents to open them. His heart function looks good overall."

Amanda sagged against the bench, her hands trembling with relief.

"Okay, so, that means he's good now, right?" Chris asked with a low voice.

"As of right now, yes. He'll be on some medications and need lifestyle changes like diet, exercise, all that. But we caught it early enough. All this information will be gone over in detail before he is discharged."

"Thank you so much, Doctor." Amanda finally found her voice.

"Of course. I'm just glad he had you there to help. We have a saying about heart attacks, time is muscle. And having you there meant he we got it quickly, and he should make a full recovery." Dr. Frank smiled at her kindly before walking away.

Chris and Amanda looked at each other. Going through the stress of this situation together made something between them shift.

The tension, anger, and confusion all melted into something quieter.

Gratitude.

Shared fear.

Relief.

"Well, want to go upstairs and find out what room he'll be in?" Chris asked gently.

"Sure BT, let me get my stuff," Amanda nodded, brushing a tear from her cheek.

She gathered her things and stood, wobbling slightly before steadying herself.

Chris couldn't help but notice how beautiful she looked, even now, with messy hair and all.

Something about her resilience made him ache.

Dangerous, he thought. Beautiful and dangerous.

They waited another hour upstairs before being allowed into Jackson's room.

He was awake, propped up in bed, oxygen tubing under his nose, with the replay of a football game blaring on the TV.

He greeted them with a tired grunt, shifting in the bed as the heart monitor beeped steadily behind him. Without missing a beat, he immediately launched into commentary about a ridiculous interception call, completely avoiding the topic of his heart attack.

"Did you see that damn interception?" he rasped, his voice scratchy but still carrying that old fire. "Ball bounced right off the receiver's fucking hands. I could've caught that drunk and blindfolded."

Amanda wiped her face quickly, forcing a breathy laugh as she slid into the chair next to his bed.

"Yeah, Dad, totally unfair," she said, her voice a little too bright. "Maybe you should call the league and give them a piece of your mind," she said, her voice wobbly but trying to sound light.

Jackson chuckled under his breath, but it faded quickly. His eyes, usually so sharp, lingered a little longer on Amanda than usual.

"You scared the hell outta me tonight, you know," Amanda blurted out before she could stop herself, her hand reaching across the bedrail to find his.

Jackson's smirk faltered. For a moment, the tough exterior slipped.

"I scared myself too, kiddo," he admitted quietly, voice still rougher than usual.

Then he squeezed her hand once, strong, reassuring and looked back up at the TV like he hadn't said anything at all.

Chris stayed leaning against the wall across the room, arms crossed, watching the two of them.

The tension in his chest loosened just slightly. Not because everything was okay, because it wasn't, but because they were still fighting to hold onto each other.

And for now, that was enough.

Amanda smiled through her tears and sat beside the bed, listening to Jackson deflect with jokes and football talk rather than acknowledging the elephant in the room. She just nodded at all the right moments.

Chris pulled a chair up, too, but he stayed a little further back, watching them both.

Jackson didn't want pity, and he didn't want to be seen as vulnerable.

And for tonight, at least, they would let him have that. As they sat together in the soft glow of the hospital room, none of them spoke about fear or loss or what might have been. They spoke only about the game on TV, pretending, just for tonight, that the world hadn't almost slipped out from under them.

Chapter 10

Amanda stared at Chris's back as he moved in the kitchen, her heart twisting with every tight, mechanical movement he made.

The house felt too big around them, too quiet, too cold—even though the spring heat still clung to the walls.

When they had finally left the hospital, she hadn't been able to face going home to an empty house. Lori would have come back over, but it wasn't the same. She needed Chris.

The way he steadied her without even trying, the way his presence anchored her when she felt like she might float away into her panic. Even after everything that had gone wrong between them tonight, he was still the one she turned to.

Chris hadn't argued much. He'd just pressed his lips together, nodded stiffly, and unlocked the Jeep. Their ride back to his house had been brutally silent. The low hum of the engine buzzed through the floorboards, filling the cabin with a cold, mechanical rhythm. Amanda stole glances at him, hoping for some kind of a sign, something human, but Chris's grip was tight on the steering wheel, his jaw tense, and his gaze locked on the empty road. By the time they pulled into his driveway, the tension between them was so thick it felt like a living thing.

Chris threw the Jeep into park with a sharp jerk, and neither of them moved or spoke.

The only sound was the tick-tick of the cooling engine and the faint rush of wind outside.

Finally, with synchronized resignation, they climbed out. The doors thudded shut with hollow, tired finality.

The short walk to the house felt endless. Amanda wrapped her arms tightly around her torso, each step heavier than the last, the humid night pressing down on her.

Inside, she barely made it to the couch before collapsing and curling into herself like she could physically hold her emotions.

Chris didn't even look at her. He moved straight for the kitchen, his movements stiff and clipped, yanking open the cabinet door hard enough that it banged against the adjacent one.

He grabbed a bottle of Highland Park 15-year single malt without hesitation, pouring a heavy two-finger measure into a glass. The amber liquid caught the light as it splashed against the sides, the smell of peat and oak drifting faintly into the room.

Amanda watched him silently, her throat tightening.

There was something violent in the way he moved. The sharp angles of his body, the contained rage simmering just beneath his skin.

Chris downed the scotch in a single smooth pull, barely wincing at the smooth finish.

His eyes stayed fixed out the window, staring into the dark backyard like he was looking for something he knew he'd never find.

With a sudden, sharp motion, he dropped the glass into the sink.

The sharp clatter of it hitting the metal was deafening in the silence, making Amanda flinch violently. She squeezed her arms tighter around herself, willing her body not to betray how shaken she felt.

Chris stood there for a moment, his shoulders heaving slightly with shallow breaths.

Then, without a word, he turned and stalked towards his room, ripping his white T-shirt off as he went. The muscles across his back tensed and shifted under his skin, a living map of barely contained fury and exhaustion.

Amanda's eyes followed him as he disappeared into his bedroom. She heard the muffled sounds of drawers opening and hangers scraping against the closet rod.

When he reappeared, he had changed into a short-sleeved button-down, the fabric hanging loose around him, still rumpled from how he'd yanked it off the hanger.

"It's too damn hot in this house," he muttered as he stomped toward the thermostat.

His voice was hoarse, low, edged with something bitter.

Amanda slowly unfolded herself from the couch, her joints stretching from the tension.

She crossed the room toward the kitchen, drawn to the sharp sound that had broken the uneasy stillness.

Peering into the sink, she found the glass resting intact among a plate and fork. It hadn't shattered. It just made a whole lot of noise.

She let out a shaky breath she hadn't realized she was holding.

"Didn't even break," she said softly, more to herself than to Chris.

Chris didn't respond.

The air conditioner kicked on with a heavy exhale through the vents, filling the house with a low, mechanical hum.

Amanda turned and leaned back against the counter, watching him.

He was leaning against the wall by the thermostat now, arms crossed tightly across his chest, head tipped back, eyes closed.

She wanted to say something. Wanted to crack through that wall he'd thrown up between them. But she didn't know where to start.

Instead, she asked the smallest thing she could think of.

A simple offering.

A peace treaty.

"You want me to wash these?" she asked quietly.

Chris cracked one eye open and looked at her.

For a moment, he just stared, like he was trying to remember how to speak to her, how to be soft.

Then he shrugged as he walked over and sank into the couch.

"Yeah... sure. Clean dishes sounds good."

He watched as Amanda stood in the kitchen washing dishes. He wanted to tell her to stop fussing with them, but he was tired and didn't want to argue. Besides, he hated washing dishes.

It wasn't forgiveness; it wasn't healing, but it was something to connect their minds.

And right now, Amanda would take anything she could get.

Chris sat on the couch with a heavy sigh, elbows on his knees, and his head hanging low. He stared at the floor, his shoulders rising and falling with each slow breath.

Amanda dried the final dish with a faded kitchen towel and turned to face him. Her gaze softened as she took him in, the way his head hung, the tension in his posture. She knew him well enough to recognize when he was retreating inward. But they couldn't keep skirting around this silence, this distance that stretched between them.

She put the dishes in the cupboard and walked over to him. Chris sat frozen on the couch, his head still buried in his hands.

"BT?" Amanda said softly, standing in front of him, but he didn't respond.

She hesitated before sinking to her knees in front of him. Gently, she wrapped her fingers around his wrists, trying to pull his hands away from his face. But his grip remained firm, his knuckles tight with tension.

"He'll be okay, BT," she said, her voice steady but tender. "The doctor said everything went well. We saw him, we talked to him, laughed about the game, remember?"

But Chris stayed silent. His mind raced with intrusive thoughts, looping fears of loss and isolation. The weight of the situation pressed heavy on his chest, suffocating and relentless. Yet, beneath the stress, something unexpected stirred, a raw and physical need he hadn't anticipated.

His breathing slowed as he glanced at Amanda. She knelt before him, her face tilted up in quiet concern. Her white tank top clung to her, framed by a cropped black corduroy jacket with her ponytail draping to one side. The rips in her jeans revealed sun-kissed skin, and her sandals gave her an air of casual softness that made his throat tighten. But it was her scent, warm, floral, and familiar, that unraveled him. It clung to the air between them, wrapping around his senses and making it hard to think.

Chris lifted his head fully and met her eyes for the first time that evening.

He firmly grabbed her wrists, careful not to hurt her. He stood up, encouraging her to stand, holding her wrists. They stood there staring at each other quietly for a moment, while he slowly lowered her arms and placed them around his waist. He bent over and kissed her on the cheek as he put his hands on her lower back.

She leaned her head back and looked up at him with a relaxed smile. She pulled him closer as he bent over to kiss her on the lips. The unexpected softness and warmth of his lips pressing against hers was the moment she wanted. The explosion of emotion, passion, and excitement was too much for her to remain calm.

Amanda pushed Chris down onto the couch. As she climbed on top of him, she began kissing him all over his face and neck. Chris made her senses go crazy. She couldn't think of anything else while she was on top of him.

She ripped his shirt open, spilling some buttons on the floor, and started kissing his chest. As her lips grazed his chest, she slowly peeled off her jacket, letting it slip to the floor like a forgotten memory. She tugged her shirt over her head with a playful flick, revealing a world of desire beneath. Rising back to meet him, her tongue danced along the sculpted lines of his muscles, igniting a fire within him. Then, with a teasing glint in her eyes, she playfully bit his bottom lip, sending waves of exhilaration through him. Chris loosened his belt, anticipation buzzing in the air as she slid down the zipper of his pants. The warmth radiating from her core enveloped his thighs, igniting a thrilling spark as she settled into his lap. With a swift brush, he unsnapped her bra, setting her beauty free and revealing her captivating breasts that took his breath away.

As Chris hungrily put each round pink nipple into his mouth and explored her curves with his hands, Amanda felt a rush of exhilaration course through her. With deliberate grace, she began to unfasten her pants, inching them down with a tantalizing slowness.

Could it be? The moment she had yearned for was finally unfolding before her.

A serendipitous encounter with the man she had always dreamed of. It was free of games and demands, pure, unfiltered chemistry that crackled in the air like a wild spark. Here they were, two souls drawn together by the magnetic pull of desire, embracing the raw, instinctive dance of attraction.

Chris was treading softly, eager to follow her rhythm, letting her set the pace.

When she finally slipped off her jeans, unveiling her lack of panties, a rush of exhilaration exploded within him. In a swift motion, he shed the last remnants of his clothes. The metallic jingle of his dog tags echoed against his muscular chest as he reclined back on the couch, heart racing. Chris's gaze roamed over her silhouette, drinking in every detail, captivated by the beauty before him. Damn, this girl is beautiful. No, this woman is beautiful. She is all grown up now, and that body has been torturing me. I need to be inside of her.

Chris reached up and pulled Amanda closer to him. They began kissing again. Her sweet tongue invaded his mouth with a blast of passion. She could feel his manhood pressing against her belly. She was leaking, and it began to run down onto his thighs. The excitement from feeling her internal juices on his thighs was exhilarating. He couldn't wait any longer. He slid his hand down between her legs and rubbed on her clit for a moment. She moaned in desire as he skillfully moved his fingers. A faint, "Ahh, yes," filled the silence not covered by their breathing.

Her essence lingered on his fingers like a tantalizing invitation that beckoned him closer. As he raised his fingers to his lips, he savored the sweetness of a dream, her flavor dancing on his tongue, while her intoxicating aroma wrapped around him like a warm embrace.

Amanda positioned herself on his engorged, throbbing, cock. She slowly started to work his meat into herself. Chris let out a grunt, "Fuck yeah," and his whole body tensed up beneath her. She could feel his breath quicken. He began pushing further inside, and her tight, warm, wet pussy was taking control of him. He had to close his eyes and curl his toes to try and keep from finishing too quickly.

Amanda was in the moment as well. The large cock was burning as he worked it in and out of her, but it felt great at the same time. She tried to whisper something sexy to him, but the words got stuck in her throat. She just leaned over and wrapped her arms around his neck as she kissed him. The dog tags jingled along with her breasts as he thrust in and out of her. The cool metal felt good against her nipples. His cock felt like it was in a warm tight glove made especially for him.

As they lost themselves in the heat of the moment, the world around them faded into a blur, leaving only the intoxicating rhythm of their bodies intertwined. Her breasts, soft and inviting, glided against his chest, creating a tantalizing friction that sent shivers of pleasure coursing through him. Each gentle bounce and subtle movement were like a siren's call, drawing him deeper into the waves of desire that enveloped them. The air was thick with a mixture of their shared warmth and the sweet, musky scent of passion that ignited an insatiable hunger within. Amanda's soft moans, barely above a whisper, resonated in Chris's ears. It was a symphony of longing, an invitation to lose himself entirely in a moment that felt both fleeting and eternal.

With each passing moment, their shared energy intensified. It created an atmosphere thick with desire and anticipation. He could feel the heat radiating from her skin. The tender, thrusting, exploration of their bodies became a language of its own, spoken in soft gasps and lingering touches. Her light laughter at the sheer surprise of it all, mingling with her moans, added a playful undertone to their intimacy, transforming the experience into something both passionate and joyful. In that cocoon of warmth and connection, they discovered not only the thrill of their physical union but also a deeper bond that was forming. It was a tapestry of shared moments woven together by thrusts, grinding, and undeniable desire.

Amanda's mouth attacked Chris's neck as she moaned louder from the orgasm that was coming. All the noises filling the room were orgasmic. Her moaning, him moaning, the dog tags clinking, grunts, and wet sounds from him pumping in and out of her squirting pussy. Sweat was trickling down her chest, onto his body. His balls began to tighten, and he started thrusting harder, faster.

"Ahh, fuck! Yes, Amanda!" Chris yelled as he pumped his warm load inside of her. He just kept pumping as his seemingly never-ending load filled her cavern. "Ohh, my God," he said as he continued to move in and out of her for a moment.

"Damn! Yes!" Amanda blurted out with her face buried in Chris's chest.

When he felt completely drained, he collapsed back on the couch. He couldn't move.

Amanda wrapped her arms back around his neck and kissed him gently, taking breaks to catch her breath. Her entire body was relaxed, and she just rested on top of him. She was enjoying smelling him, touching his sweaty skin, listening to him breathe, and watching the rise and fall of his chiseled chest.

After a few minutes, she sat up and rolled beside him. They both turned sideways so they could fit on the couch together.

Amanda glanced at him, as he seemed to be in deep thought. And his face was telling her that his thoughts were not good.

Chris started to get a sick feeling in the pit of his stomach. He sat up and began looking for his clothes.

LT is in the hospital, and here I am fucking his daughter. The little girl of my friend. I have to get the fuck out of here. I just need a minute to think, Chris thought as he gave up looking for his clothes in the dark living room, got up, and walked to the bedroom. He didn't say a word to Amanda. He just left her there on the couch in a leftover puddle of their desire.

What the fuck was that about? Amanda thought as she couldn't believe he had just left her again.

In the bedroom, he put on a new white shirt, gray sweatpants, and some Jordan sneakers. As Chris emerged from the bedroom, Amanda asked, "Did I do something wrong this time, too? I mean, you started it this time."

Now she was sitting up with her knees pulled toward her chest and both arms resting over her breasts.

"Umm, no. I...uhh, fuck where are my keys?"

When he responded, he didn't even look at her; he just kept searching for his keys.

As tears strolled down her face, Amanda pulled on her white tank top and ripped jeans. She was starting to feel the pain of embarrassment in her stomach again. Truthfully, she just wanted to go to the bathroom and cry in private.

Chris was still frantically searching around for his keys when he heard her start to cry. He could feel her eyes on him, but he needed some air, space, and time.

"You know, we didn't do anything wrong. I'm an adult and this is exactly what I wanted. I loved having you inside of me." Amanda said as she sat on the couch wiping her tears. Her arms folded across her chest as she waited hopefully for a response this time.

"How the hell did they get back there?" Chris said as he found the keys behind the TV. "This shouldn't have happened," he finally replied to her statement. "I get what you're saying, but...it just shouldn't have happened."

"Well, I'm glad it did happen. I've been wanting this for a long time. I even planned it out earlier," she said as she stood up from her perch. Amanda walked over to him and put her arms around his waist. He didn't move or push her away.

"Well, this is a start," she thought with a smile.

She looked up into his eyes, those wonderfully inviting light brown eyes of his, and he looked down at her. At that moment, she knew this was who she wanted to be with; she loved him and felt that he should know.

"Chris..." After a long pause, close to a minute, she continued. "Chris, I love you. And... and I know you'll think it's just—" was all she got out before he started pushing her away.

"No, no, no, nope... don't... don't do that. Just, please don't do that," he said and walked away from her. He stood by the door, looking into nothingness.

"You need to go. I'll take you home or back to the hospital, but you can't stay here."

"I'm not going anywhere until we talk, BT!" Amanda said, raising her voice.

"What do you want to talk about?" Chris asked in a more irritated voice.

"I—" was all she got out before he cut her off.

"I fucking came in you. Ohh fuck! Please tell me that you're on birth control because I definitely came in you."

"Yes!" she said, staring at him for a few moments. "Is that seriously the only thing you have to say to me? After that wonderful moment together, what the fuck?"

"Shit, what are we doing here? I mean seriously!" he shouted as he jerked the door open and walked out.

Amanda was confused and beginning to get angry.

"What the hell is your problem?" She shouted to the open door as she started to angrily chuckle at the situation. "Why are you acting like such a bitch right now?"

With no reply from outside, she shook her head in confusion, walked out, and slammed the door closed this time.

She slammed the door so hard the whole house rattled, the echo crashing back at her louder than she'd expected.

Amanda stood there for a moment, frozen, her back pressed to the house, the reality of what had just happened crashing down around her.

The night had unraveled faster than she could process.

She was in his arms one moment, tangled in yearning, sweat, and moans whispered in the dark.

The next, he had ripped himself away from her like she was something he needed to escape.

Her heart ached in her chest, a dull, squeezing pain that only got worse as the silence around her thickened.

She leaned her head against the door, shutting her eyes tight.

Tears she thought she'd run out of began to spill down her cheeks again, hot and angry.

I gave him everything, she thought bitterly. I gave him all of me. And he still ran.

She wiped her face roughly with the back of her hand and pushed herself away from the door.

Her whole body trembled, not from fear or from sadness but from a deep, searing humiliation she couldn't shake.

Her body still smelled faintly of him, of sweat and sex and her broken hopes for a magical ending. Just moments ago, she had felt safe... loved... seen.

Now, it felt cold.

Now, she felt foolish.

He thinks this was a mistake, but it wasn't. Not for me, she thought.

And despite the ache in her chest, she knew one thing with certainty:

She still loved him.

Even if he hated himself for loving her back.

Chapter 11

Back at the hospital, Chris and Amanda sat in the waiting area, two chairs apart, both staring into the middle distance as if afraid of eye contact.

The air between them was thick and unmoving like the sterile cream walls pressing in around them.

From around the corner, a cheerful voice cut through the silence.

"Hey, Branson family?"

Amanda stood first, snapping to attention. "Yes, that's me and him, I guess."

The nurse smiled. Her badge read Brenda, RN. "Great. You can come in now. Only two people at a time, though."

Amanda gave a slight nod, her face tight, and followed Brenda down the hallway. Chris trailed behind them in silence, his footsteps stiff and mechanical.

As they entered Jackson's room, they found him sitting upright in bed, tablet in hand, glasses perched on the end of his nose. He looked up, his face lighting with a familiar warmth.

"You two were just in here," Jackson said with a smirk, pulling off his glasses. "I told you I'm fine. It's okay to leave."

"Yeah, but we wanted to make sure they were treating you okay," Chris replied, forcing a smile.

"I don't want you two worrying about me. I'm going to be just fine," Jackson said, waving a hand. "Honestly, I'm ready to go home. This place is driving me nuts. It's just beeping monitors, no late-night food, and people farting through the walls. You ever heard an old man cough-fart through a wall at 0100? I have now."

Chris chuckled. "Sounds like paradise."

"Hopefully you'll be out tomorrow," Amanda added quietly, barely above a whisper.

She stood near the foot of the bed, eyes fixed on the IV in Jackson's arm like it held the answer to some question she wasn't ready to ask. She refused to look at Chris.

Despite the dull ache in his chest and the heaviness from the procedure, Jackson noticed everything.

Amanda wouldn't meet Chris's eyes.

Chris hadn't stopped glancing at the floor since they walked in.

Something's up, he thought. Something's not right here.

He shifted in bed, scratching the back of his neck. "Amanda, could you get me some ice?"

"Sure. Where's the machine?"

"Around the corner from the nurses' station, I think. If you get lost, just ask the desk."

"Okay." She offered a polite smile and slipped out of the room.

The second the door clicked shut, Chris exhaled like he'd been holding his breath the entire time.

Jackson narrowed his eyes at him.

"So... any cute nurses on this floor?" Chris asked, trying for casual, though his voice came out too fast and forced.

Jackson didn't bite.

"Is everything okay?"

Chris straightened a little, nodding. "Yes, sir. Just... you being in the hospital. It caught both of us off guard. You're never sick. I mean, not really. Just those sniffles on Christmas a few years ago and the stomach bug you had that almost killed the plumbing with explosive shits."

Jackson gave a short laugh but didn't break his stare.

"She sure seemed fine earlier when she came by. Now she won't even look at you."

Chris hesitated. The air between them tensed like a wire about to snap.

Before he could answer, the door opened again.

Amanda walked in holding a small plastic pitcher of ice, her eyes flicking between the two men. She immediately noticed the silence.

"Did I interrupt something?" she asked, trying to keep her voice light.

"Just some man talk," Jackson said smoothly, accepting the ice from her. "Thanks, sweetheart."

Chris cleared his throat and straightened his shirt. "Well... I'm gonna head home. Do you want me to drop you off?"

Amanda's smile was polite, tight at the corners. "No, that's okay. I'll call Lori. She wanted to come visit Dad."

Chris nodded. "Alrighty then."

He turned to Jackson and raised a hand. "Take care, LT. I'll check on you tomorrow."

Jackson returned the wave but said nothing.

As Chris walked past Amanda toward the hallway, he didn't meet her eyes. His jaw was tight, and his footsteps were quick.

Fuck, he thought as he passed the nurses' station, the sterile lights above him buzzing faintly.

Back in the room, Amanda watched the door long after Chris left.

"Do you think BT is acting strange?" Jackson asked, trying not to let the doubt in his voice show.

Amanda raised an eyebrow. "No. He seemed fine in the waiting area earlier. Quiet. Sitting alone."

"Right..." Jackson nodded. But he wasn't convinced.

He turned toward the window, ice slowly melting in the cup beside him.

Jackson had known Chris a long time and Amanda even longer. Something had changed between them, and whether they admitted to it or not, it was only a matter of time before things came spilling out.

*****

Chris pulled into his driveway after taking the long way home, windows cracked, the humid night air rolling over his face as if it might wash away the guilt. The street was quiet, except the engine ticking faintly as it cooled. He stayed in the Jeep, hands gripping the wheel, eyes unfocused. He sat there for a few minutes, ruminating on the day's events. It felt good having Amanda wrapped around his waist, and the sex was amazing. The way she moved on top of him, confident, hungry, unafraid. It was a side of her he'd never seen. For a while, he always viewed her as timid and off-limits. She had been the sweet, shy daughter of his closest friend. But that night...her being on top of him changed everything. A smile came across his face as he continued to reminisce about the intense moment.

However, his smile quickly gave way to worry.

I had sex with LT's daughter. What the fuck. He imagined Jackson's voice in his head, low and calm, "Some shit, you can't walk back from, Temple."

He now felt horrible about his decision, again. Chris blew out a long breath, dragged himself out of the Jeep, and walked into the house, shoulders heavy. Chris dropped to the couch and tossed his keys on the floor. His entire body was exhausted. The stress of the evening finally caught up to him. He reached for the TV remote, and Amanda's scent hit him like a sucker punch from the couch cushion. He leaned in without thinking and breathed it in. His cock stirred immediately.

"Damn," he muttered, pushing his head back into the cushion.

"She's too young for me. Besides, she doesn't really know what she wants. What the hell am I doing? I mean she is an adult, and we're not related," Chris thought as he tried to rationalize the situation. He had been a family friend for a long time and treated her like a little sister. But his body didn't care. His memory didn't care. And the guilt? It had set up shop right in his gut.

"This is going to be hard as fuck. I hope she understands, but I gotta stay away from her. No contact whatsoever. I just hope I'm strong enough to do it, because that was, amazing."

* * * * *

Three weeks had passed since Amanda and Chris last saw each other. It was the longest she had ever gone without seeing him unless he was deployed. He wasn't deployed this time, and she realized he was purposefully avoiding her. Chris used to come to the house multiple times a week for as long as she had known him.

Since being released from the hospital, Jackson had spent most of his time in the study. Chris would talk over the phone or video chat to check up on him. Jackson pretended that it was normal for Chris not to come over for this long and to use video chat for anything. Amanda was also pretending everything was normal, but inside it was tearing her apart.

She had thoughts about driving over to his house many times. She wanted to kiss him and tell him everything would be okay. Their first time together was special, and it still made her wet thinking about being on top of him, sweating and thrusting. His perfectly toned brown body was between her legs.

Thoughts of Chris being with April had entered her mind. "Maybe she's more experienced than me. Could it be that the sex wasn't good?" She had tried to get those thoughts out of her mind, but it kept coming back. "He felt so good though. If I can just get a second chance, I know I can make it better. Damn I just miss him so much."

While Amanda did miss Chris, she was not going to wait around for him anymore.

[Friday night a few weeks later]

Amanda stared at the full-length mirror in her room, holding a pair of nude heels in one hand and black strappy ones in the other. She tossed both onto the bed and sat down with a sigh. Her phone buzzed. A text from Lori:

Tonight isn't anything permanent. You don't have to prove a thing. Just have fun, bitch.

But I do, Amanda thought as she chuckled at Lori's message.

She'd thought about driving over to Chris's house a dozen times. Standing at his door and saying what needed to be said. That their time together meant something. That she wasn't just some one-night mistake. But every time she reached for her keys, she froze. Chris hadn't texted. Hadn't called. Not even a damn emoji.

She'd drafted a message earlier that day, something short, flirty.

Hey stranger. I miss you. I still think about that night...

She deleted it before she finished typing.

Now, her short black dress hugged her curves just right, her lipstick was flawless, and the gold necklace at her collarbone shimmered against her skin. She looked like she had moved on.

But her chest was tight with disappointment when she looked through the window and didn't see Chris's Jeep.

Amanda was in the living room waiting on her date, Brendan. Brendan had asked Amanda for a date a few months ago, but she declined because Chris was her focus. Lori had tried to talk her into going out with other guys and still pursue Chris, but Amanda was not having that. However, since Chris wanted to use the stay-away strategy, she decided to do the same and try to move on. Thus, she finally accepted Brendan's request for a date. They were going to see a movie, get drinks and dinner at The Garden Room, and head to his friend's house afterward.

There was a knock at the door. Knowing that it was most likely Brendan, Amanda was hopeful that it was Chris instead. She looked through the side glass and saw Brendan. Happy to see Brendan, she was still a little disappointed it wasn't Chris.

"You look incredible," Brendan said as she opened the door.

"Thank you. It's just something I threw together," Amanda said with a smile.

She was wearing a short black strapless dress with black heels. She had her gold pillar bar necklace on, with gold earrings. Her hair was pinned up with a pink flower on the side. She had a splash of Dior perfume behind her ears. Brendan wore a dark green polo shirt, khakis, and dark Oxfords.

Amanda got into the car and asked, "Well, is this going to be an action movie or scary movie?"

"You will just have to wait and see," Brendan said with a wink.

They pulled into the crowded theater lot and eventually found a parking space. Brendan hopped out of the car and ran around to open Amanda's door. She stepped out and read, "Dead Life 3," on the marquee.

Uhh, a horror movie, she moaned to herself.

She was never a big fan of them in public because she was scared so easily. Now, Brendan was going to see how she reacted to horror movies.

They walked up and had to stand in line because Brendan didn't get tickets before they arrived. Brendan covertly put his arm around her waist as they waited. Amanda wasn't crazy about his smooth move but didn't ask him to remove it.

He scanned the number of people in front of them.

"I hope we get tickets," he said.

"Well, I'm just wondering why you didn't get them online since it's a new movie?"

"Online? No, they charge like five dollars for a service fee per ticket. I wasn't paying that," he said with a smile.

Ohh, perfect, he's fucking cheap, she thought.

"Amanda," a deep voice whispered near her ear.

"Ahh shit!" yelled Amanda as she covered her mouth to muffle the scream from being startled.

Her eyes widened, and she quickly turned to see where the voice was coming from. Her eyes narrowed as she saw, there he was. Chris stood in a dark blue vintage tee shirt, black South Carolina baseball cap, denim jeans, and cowboy boots.

"Damn, he looks so sexy," Amanda thought silently, but her lips still mouthed the words. The cap cast a shadow over his face, obscuring his expression. His voice in her ear, whispering her name, made her body tingle.

Chris saw them when they walked up to get in line. At first glance, it appeared as though they were just friends, that is, until he put his arm around her waist. That display made Chris see red. He was upset to see someone else touching her like that, but conversely, being upset about it irritated him. Things were the way they should be. This guy was her age, and she needed to have an enjoyable life. However, this high-level thinking still showed fissures of jealousy, as Chris wanted to smack Brendan to the ground.

Earlier in the day, Chris and Darren were relaxing at his house, drinking and watching a replay of Super Bowl LII. After drinking all day, they decided to get more active and played basketball at the gym. The onion rings, beer, and chicken wings did not mix well with a pickup basketball game. Five minutes into the first game, they both retched into the trash can near the door.

"Okay, this was a stupid fucking idea, Darren."

"Yeah, I think we're done man. Let's head back to the house."

"Good call. I need to brush my teeth. I can feel the grit on my molars." Chris said with a laugh.

They grabbed their bags from the locker room and left.

"That gym damn near killed me," Darren groaned as he sat on Chris's couch. "Remind me why we thought beer, wings, and hoops was a good idea?"

Chris grinned. "Because we're idiots."

They laughed and clinked bottles like battle-worn survivors.

After a while, Darren kicked his feet up. "Hey man, you been kinda off lately."

Chris rolled his eyes but didn't answer.

"I mean I'm not the best at talking about shit sometimes, but I listen," Darren continued.

"I feel fine. I guess I've just been tired. Shit, man I don't know."

Darren thought briefly, "Maybe you need a hug or something. Just need to cry it out."

Chris laughed heavily, "Yo, shut the fuck up. Some great listener you are."

"Hey, I do what I can," Darren said with a laugh.

After being home for a while, Darren perked up.

"Hey man, you want to see that new horror movie?"

"Yeah, sure. Beats the hell out of staying at the house all day," Chris replied.

That evening, they decided on the new theater in town, which had large leather recliners. They changed, hopped into Chris's Jeep, and drove towards the theater.

"Hey, did you get the tickets yet?"

"Nah, I don't wanna download the app. Let's just jump in line. I'm sure it won't be too busy," Darren responded.

As they pulled into the parking lot, Chris gave Darren a death stare as they looked over the busy lot for a parking space.

"See, yeah, I told you. It won't be busy at all," Darren said with a laugh. "Okay, okay. So, clearly I was wrong. Just fucking park already."

Finally, they found a space, and the Jeep lurched to a stop. They hopped out and talked as they walked up to get in line. Chris was getting frustrated waiting in line. He was about to tell Darren they should try another place, but then he saw Amanda. She looked amazing in her dress, and he couldn't take his eyes off her. Her dress showed off those legs he'd memorized, the sight, the feel, and the strength of having them squeeze around his waist.

Darren eventually saw her, too.

"Hey, Amanda's over there. We should go speak."

"Yeah, sure. Let's go," Chris quickly agreed.

He had his jaw clenched, and his feet moved before he told them to. Darren barely had time to follow before Chris cut through the line, ignoring the grumbles from strangers.

When they got behind her, Chris stood staring at the back of her neck for a moment. Her hair was pinned up, and the smell of her perfume filled his lungs. He could feel the fire within him burn brighter as he stared. His mind drifted back several weeks to when he was kissing that very neck, and that same scent coated his chest and couch. Those thoughts quickly left his mind as his eyes scanned down and saw Brendan's arm around her waist. He wanted to break Brendan's arm off but resisted that brief bout of jealousy. Instead, he decided to whisper her name. Plus, by getting in close, he could feel her warmth again.

Amanda examined Chris's face as he looked from her face to Brendan's arm numerous times.

"Hello Chris," she said calmly. Amanda then turned to Darren, "And hello to you too, Darren."

Darren started to pick up on a weird vibe with the situation, as his face showed uneasiness. "Uhh...hey Amanda," Darren replied before Chris.

"Yeah, hey there Amanda. How are you doing?" Chris asked, trying to force a smile.

"I'm good. Ohh, umm...this is Brendan," she stated as Brendan cleared his throat and stared at the two guys.

Brendan reached up to fist bump Darren's hand, and he reached out to accept the gesture. He attempted to do the same with Chris as he turned to him, but Chris never took his eyes off Amanda. After a few seconds, Brendan put his hand down.

"It's like that, huh?" he said to Chris as a statement but didn't get a reply.

The silence between them was interrupted by the cashier.

"Can I help you folks?" she asked irritatedly.

Amanda exhaled sharply and turned toward the ticket window.

He's mad. He's jealous. Good. But even as she thought it, her chest was aching for him.

"Yes, sorry. Two for Dead Life 3," Amanda replied. As she was about to pay, Brendan stopped her hand as to say no, then raised his phone to use his tap to pay.

"I got it all day. Don't want my baby to have to pay for anything this evening," he said, smiling at her.

Darren began to chuckle because Brendan placed emphasis on 'baby.' Brendan heard the chuckle and moved his arm up around Amanda's shoulder as they walked into the theater. Chris stood there for a few seconds, contemplating many ways to hurt that young man. That little asshole is so lucky, he thought.

"What's wrong man? You two mad at each other about something?" Darren asked.

"No, nothing. Let's just go. I got these, you get the beer," said Chris as he took the tickets and walked inside.

Amanda was trying to avoid looking at the theater entrance. Still, she was curious if Chris and Darren were going to the same movie as them. She quickly found out, yes, as they walked in and up the aisle. She lost sight of them as they walked to the back of the theater. Badly, she wanted to turn and look for Chris. But Brendan was watching her.

"So, who were those guys in line?"

"Hmm, ohh, they work with my dad. Well, they used to work with him in the Navy," she said, feigning aloofness.

"Cool, cool. Well, why was that one just staring at you like that? I think his name was Chad."

"No, that was Chris. I don't really know, I haven't seen him weeks," she said as she pulled her phone out.

The thoughts of everything were making her anxious and sending random thoughts through her head. "Okay, he was staring and trying to be nice. So, what. Fuck him, he had me feeling terrible for weeks and ignored me." The thoughts of his actions replaced her anxiousness with anger. She decided to be strong like her dad had taught her.

The lights dimmed, and coming attractions started to play. Amanda was trying to concentrate on the previews, but she was thirsty.

"Hey, Brendan, I'm going to get a Coke. Want anything?"

Brendan shook his head, no, without looking at her, as he was engrossed in the current preview for a superhero movie. Amanda got up and quickly walked out to the concession stand without looking for Chris as she left.

The temperature in the lobby was much cooler than in the theater. Still, that could have more to do with her nerves than the ambient temperature. She decided to take a trip to the women's restroom before getting a drink. Looking in the mirror as she walked into the bathroom to check her makeup, she still looked good despite sweating a bit. While using the restroom, she heard some young girls giggle as they walked out. She opened her stall and screamed. Immediately covering her mouth to muffle the sound. There was Chris leaning casually with his back to her, against the wall.

Chapter 12

Amanda walked to the sink and looked in the mirror again as she washed her hands, remaining silent. The bathroom smelled faintly of industrial cleaner and buttered popcorn. The clashing scents did nothing to settle the butterflies in her stomach. She tried to pretend that Chris didn't matter. He turned and watched as she looked in the mirror, fixing her hair. He had told Darren that he was going to buy a drink seconds before Amanda got up from her seat. When he saw her run into the bathroom, he decided to follow her and wait.

"You know this is the women's restroom," she said with one hand leaning on the sink, looking irritated.

"Yeah, I learned to read a while ago, ya know?" he answered as he continued to stare.

Looking at Chris this close started to make Amanda's heartbeat speed up. She thought, "Shit, I need to get out of here. I can't trust myself around him."

She started to walk around him to leave, and he reached his hand out towards her. She slowly reached up to grab it, against her better judgment. He slowly pulled her closer to him. She stepped between his legs and placed both of her hands on his chest. She was about to push him away, but he leaned in and kissed her softly on the lips. The kiss sent waves of ecstasy through her body. Her head started to spin with thoughts of him, good thoughts of him.

She was trying hard to remember why she was mad. Then it came to her, "No, he fucked me, made me feel like garbage, and then ignored me for weeks."

Finally, with those thoughts raging back, Amanda pushed him away.

"You have no right to kiss me like that! I'm on a date right now, and I need to get back to him." She said in a raised voice.

"Look, I'm sorry, but you didn't say anything when I went in for the kiss. I went slowly. Besides, what the hell do you see in this guy anyway," Chris shouted back.

"What I see is a guy that knows what he wants. He wanted me, asked me out, and there were no questions in his mind about that."

"Ohh, fucking great for him, let's have a round of applause." He clapped sarcastically. "Look, the situation with us is different. He didn't spend years treating you like a little sister, and you're not a daughter to someone he viewed as a father figure."

"Is that all you can think about? I–am–a–grown–woman, okay, Chris!" she said in a loud, slow statement. "If you want me, then do something about it. Otherwise, fuck off!"

As she backed up to leave, he placed his hands on both sides of her face and began kissing her hard. Her statement was the impetus he needed to unleash his weeks of frustration. He kissed the side of her neck, then pulled the top of her dress down, exposing her strapless bra and kissing lower. He pulled the bra down with one hand as he kept rubbing her thighs with the other. Her beautiful, plump, round breasts with reddish nipples were just begging to be in his mouth. He eagerly took a nipple in his mouth and sucked.

Amanda let out a moan, "Yes, yes." She couldn't think straight. What he was doing felt so good, and she didn't want him to stop. He then took one hand and reached under her dress. His hand reached her wet pussy with ease as she wasn't wearing any panties. His long, thick fingers began probing her sweet spot. She grabbed his head as he was fingering her. His pants began to tent from the arousal of feeling her. He moved lower on her body with his mouth, pulling her dress up. He stuck his tongue directly into her throbbing pussy.

"Oh fuck," she moaned. "Here, let's go in that big stall."

"Good idea," Chris said with a chuckle as he removed his face from between her legs.

They pushed the door closed inside the stall and latched it with a loud clank. Chris pushed Amanda against the wall and continued to work his tongue inside of her as she leaned her head back. Her legs started to feel weak as he reached up and played with her nipples. Chris continued his tongue quest inside of her.

"Ohh yes. Ohh yes, BT please don't stop. I'm cumming," she said right before her explosion flowed into his mouth.

Chris continued to lick her clean. He loved her amazing taste, but he wanted to be inside her now. He stood up and unbuckled his pants. As he pulled them down, his cock sprang out. Amanda reached out and pulled him closer to her with his cock. Her small soft hands felt great wrapped around his dick. He pushed her against the wall harder as he stepped between her legs. In one motion, he had her legs wrapped around him, up on the railing in the stall. Amanda put her arms around his neck, and he leaned in for a kiss, savoring the action.

Chris reached down and placed his stiff rod right at her opening. He slipped all the way inside of her, and they both moaned.

"Damn, you're so tight and warm," Chris whispered as he began to thrust in and out. She tightened her grip on his neck and began to rub the back of it. He pumped faster and harder. They heard someone briefly come into the bathroom, but they left after hearing the moans and wet sloshing with each thrust. They were not about to stop.

"Amanda, you feel so good. Damn, baby," he whispered into her mouth.

"Uhh, you do too BT," she said excitedly.

Chris started kissing her neck while pumping into her harder. There was another rise coming to Amanda, and she started grabbing at his muscular arms.

"Yes...yes...harder," she squeaked. Chris continued to batter her warm insides. "I'm cumming again. You better not stop. Fuck!" He put his hand over her mouth to stifle the sound.

Chris could feel her burst of wetness surround his cock, and with that, he released his warm load.

"Ohh, shit baby," he said through clenched teeth as he pushed his load deep inside of her.

He stood there for a moment holding her, as his shaft continued to pulsate and spray her insides. He finally let her down from the rail, as her legs were shaking.

Amanda felt drunk on passion for a moment. She couldn't see straight, her body was tingling, and her ears were ringing. This man drove her wild, but she wanted to kick herself for letting him get to her like that.

They both were silently looking into each other's eyes. No words, just heavy, relieved breathing.

Once she finally got hold of her senses, she pushed him away. Amanda pulled her bra up and the dress down as she walked out of the stall. Her walk to the mirror was wobbly, as her legs were still tingling from the quick rendezvous.

"Well sir, you sure know how to make a woman feel special. First you treat me like some random at your house, now we fuck in a dirty bathroom. Thanks guy."

Chris tried to act like the comment didn't hurt him. He pulled up his pants and fixed his clothes.

"Could you hand me some paper?" Amanda called out, not looking at him.

"Why?"

"Because I want to clean myself up a bit. They only have the air dryer," she responded in an irritated voice.

"Just so you can go be with that guy?"

"If I want to then yes. I can be with whomever I want, Chris," she said with an emphasis on the Ch.

"Look, you can't be with him."

Amanda turned quickly with that statement.

"Can't, did you say can't? I do not belong to anyone, and if I did it sure as hell wouldn't be you. Not after what you pulled. Man, Fuck You!"

Chris still wasn't ready to have this conversation with her, but he knew he had to at this point.

"Look, I was scared okay. I wanted you so bad, but your father would hate me for it. I thought staying away from you would fix the problem, but here we are again. I even followed you and Lori last week at the mall for a little while, just to see you."

Her face softened towards him, and a smile started to form. This was a bit of a turn-on for her.

"Basically, it's like this," Chris continued as he stepped closer. "I can't stay away from you and be okay. I tried, that shit don't work," he said as he leaned down to kiss her softly.

After a few more tender kisses, they finally broke apart. Amanda's heart was pounding for reasons beyond lust, now. She began to feel guilt, fear, and confusion. She rested her forehead against Chris's chest for a moment, exhaling slowly.

"Come on, we better get out of here," she whispered, her voice still breathless as she laced her fingers with his.

They stepped out of the restroom, trying to look casual, but Amanda's pulse was racing.

As they exited into the glowing arcade-lit lobby of the theater, Amanda immediately spotted Brendan leaning against a tall racing game, arms crossed, scanning the room like a hawk. His eyes landed on them and on their interlocked hands. His face darkened with slow, simmering rage.

Amanda froze, and Chris slowed his pace beside her. She felt the air shift again, but it wasn't romantic this time; it was thick with tension.

Brendan pushed off the machine, his shoes scraping against the tile floor as he started walking toward them.

Chris instinctively stepped in front of Amanda just slightly, not to shield her, but to intercept whatever was coming. His jaw tightened, and Amanda could almost hear the calculations spinning in his head.

Across the lobby, Darren stood near the new movie cutout, watching. Chris's eyes met his friend's, and they exchanged a quick, silent message. He saw. Shit. He definitely saw us leave the bathroom. I'm going to have to come clean with him.

Brendan stopped about two feet away from them, his arms no longer crossed, hands now clenched into fists at his sides.

"So, Amanda, it's like that?" he said, voice taut, like a guitar string on the verge of snapping.

She took a cautious step forward, guilt crawling up her spine. "Brendan, look, I'm sorry, okay? I didn't mean to leave like that. I just... I needed a minute, and—"

Brendan didn't even blink at her apology. His eyes were locked on Chris.

Chris didn't flinch or blink. His face was stone cold, unreadable.

"You ran out on me for this trash-ass dude?" Brendan spat, gesturing at Chris like he was something rotting in the sun.

Chris let out a low chuckle. It wasn't playful, it was menacing.

"What the fuck are you laughing at, bitch?" Brendan snapped, stepping forward.

Chris's smile widened just slightly, like a wolf baring its teeth. "I'm laughing at your clown ass. Who the fuck else you think I'm looking at?"

Amanda's chest tightened. This was escalating fast. Too fast.

Across the lobby, Darren exhaled loudly and started moving toward them, muttering, "Here we go."

"Bitch, I'll end you," Brendan growled, puffing his chest.

"Isn't it past your bedtime, son?" Chris replied, tilting his head.

Amanda didn't know what to do, but she could tell that neither of them was too keen on backing down. She stepped between them, pushing lightly on Chris's chest. "Hey. Hey! There's no need for this."

She turned to Brendan. "Brendan, I'll pay you back for the tickets, okay? I'm sorry. I never meant to..."

"And fuck you too. Dirty-ass bitch. I don't need nothing from you." Brendan cut her off with a venom-laced snarl.

Chris's expression changed instantly.

He stepped forward, slowly, like a predator sizing up prey. Darren was now beside him, one hand out, ready to hold him back.

"You got one more time to call her out of her name like that," Chris said, his voice lower, flat, and dangerous.

Amanda's heart was thudding so hard she could barely hear anything else. Her fingers trembled as she reached for Chris's arm, trying to calm the storm.

"Come on," she urged quietly. "You've started enough shit tonight. Let's just go. Please."

Chris looked like he might take her advice. His shoulders relaxed just slightly as she began to pull him away. Then Brendan opened his mouth again.

"Don't worry about me. I just wanted to fuck anyway. Heard you were a good little cum dumpster."

The words echoed louder than they should have, and it seemed like everything happened in slow motion.

Chris turned so fast that it was like time skipped a frame. The first hit came like a gunshot, an uppercut to Brendan's gut that folded him in half. Before Brendan could even gasp for air, Chris's fist hooked hard into his jaw. The sound of it cracked through the lobby like a thunderclap.

Brendan collapsed to the floor like a dropped sack of bricks, blood pouring from his mouth, a tooth skidding across the tile.

Amanda gasped, hands flying to her mouth.

"And stay down, you little shit!" Chris barked, standing over him, chest heaving.

Darren grabbed Chris from behind, locking his arms around his shoulders and yanking him back. "BT, what the fuck!? You know what happens if we get caught fighting in public like this!"

Chris struggled for a second, adrenaline still roaring through him, before letting Darren pull him away. His eyes never left Brendan's crumpled form on the ground.

Amanda stood frozen, dumbfounded. The lobby around them had quieted. A few onlookers stood back near the concession stand, pulling out their phones and watching with wide eyes and popcorn bags halfway raised.

She didn't know whether to kneel down and help Brendan or follow Chris and Darren. Her feet refused to move.

"Amanda, bring your ass on, now!" Darren called over his shoulder.

Chris was already heading toward the exit, Darren still gripping his arm.

Amanda snapped out of it.

"Okay! Okay, I'm coming!"

She took one last look at Brendan, who was groaning and trying to roll over, before hurrying out of the theater.

The cool air outside hit her like a slap. Chris was already in the driver's seat of his Jeep, engine growling. Darren jumped into the passenger seat, breathing heavily.

"Goddamn," he muttered. "We're definitely banned from that theater."

Amanda climbed into the back seat; the door slamming shut behind her. No one said a word as Darren scanned for police. Chris threw the Jeep into the drive and screeched out of the parking lot.

The adrenaline was still thick in the air. It was hot, wild, and reckless.

Chris kept one hand on the wheel, the other tapping his thigh restlessly. Amanda noticed how he kept glancing at her through the rearview mirror. She didn't know what to say. She wasn't even sure what she felt.

Meanwhile, Darren looked at Chris from the corner of his eye. He also noticed that Chris kept eyeing Amanda in the mirror.

Chris was going well over the speed limit, racing through the night toward Darren's house. The tension in the Jeep was thick, and no one was speaking. There was just the low rumble of the engine and the occasional screech of tires on sharp turns.

Finally, they pulled up to Darren's driveway. Chris hit the brakes, and the Jeep came to a sudden, jerking stop. Darren leaned forward, resting his arm on the dashboard.

Darren got out and looked at Amanda in the back with a half-smile.

"Well, it's been an...eventful evening young lady. See you around, okay."

"Yeah, see you Darren."

Then he looked at Chris, and the two silently stared at each other for a second. Chris didn't need to hear it aloud to know what Darren was thinking, "You're a fucking idiot."

Darren gave him a slight nod, a smirk tugging at the corner of his mouth as he stepped away from the Jeep and shut the door.

"See you later, BT," he yelled over his shoulder as he walked up the steps and disappeared into the house.

Chris sat there for a moment, the engine idling and hands still gripping the wheel. The adrenaline was finally wearing off, leaving behind a strange quiet.

He glanced up at the rearview mirror, catching Amanda's eyes.

"You can come sit up front if you want," he said, his voice softer now. "I don't bite... unless asked."

A small smile tugged at Amanda's lips. She rolled her eyes and climbed over the center console into the passenger seat. Chris watched her settle in before shifting the Jeep into drive and pulling back onto the street.

For a few minutes, neither of them spoke. The streetlights passed in soft glows, their reflections dancing across the windshield.

Amanda finally broke the silence.

"So... my dad thinks I'm still with Brendan," she said casually, glancing over at him. "The movie's not over yet, and we were supposed to hit a party after."

Chris raised an eyebrow, doing the math in his head. "So that gives you, what—three hours?"

"Give or take." She smirked. "Now, what do you think a grown woman and a grown man could do to pass the time?"

Chris stole a glance at her, his mouth twitching into a grin. "I'm sure we could... schedule something."

Amanda chuckled and leaned over, pressing a soft kiss to his cheek.

"Let's go to your place and relax."

Chris's smile deepened as he turned down the next road. No more questions. No more second-guessing. Just the two of them and a few borrowed hours.

Chapter 13

Amanda was standing in Chris's bathroom as she reached up to pull the hair clip from the mess atop her head. Her hair fell over her shoulders, cascading in soft, relaxed waves. She shook it out, then carefully removed the flower from earlier. A tiny sigh escaped her lips. The bathroom smelled faintly of his cologne, something woodsy and masculine. The scent curled around her like an invisible hand. As she opened the mirrored cabinet, a box of Skyn condoms tumbled out and hit the sink with a dull thud. Amanda jumped slightly with a gasp, then stared at the box.

"At least he's safe with other women, I guess. Asshole," she muttered, lips curling in a half-sneer.

She picked up the box and turned it over in her hand, not sure what she was hoping to find. An expiration date? A note? Her first reaction was positive, with annoyance mixed in. But beneath that was something messier.

"Who is he using these with anyway? Definitely not me." She thought as she bit the inside of her cheek. This wasn't jealousy, not exactly. It was the creeping awareness that she wasn't the first but was hopefully the last. The sting of curiosity was flickering in her chest.

"Not my business," she murmured, even though it felt like it was. She put the box back in the cabinet and then walked out of the bathroom.

Outside the door, she found Chris leaning against the wall in the hallway, seemingly deep in thought, and he turned to look at her. He walked over and kissed her on the forehead, then her lips. His hands caressed the sides of her face as he stared down into her eyes.

I wonder if she knows how gorgeous she is.

Amanda, with a smile and head tilt, lifted her hand for Chris to kiss it. He grabbed her hand, kissed it, and lightly pulled her toward his bedroom.

His room always had an order to it, even if it wasn't completely neat. Everything had a place in the corners, drawers, and the desk. His bed was turned down, with military corners. Amanda assumed it was because of his military career.

"I wish I could have made love to you on a bed first," he said as he looked into her eyes.

"Well, the world is full of firsts. It just depends on how you choose to look at it," Amanda replied as he was kissing her neck.

Every part of her was so soft, and her skin smelled like vanilla mixed with lavender. Amanda pushed Chris onto the bed. She rubbed his head, then moved on to removing the shirt and jeans. Deciding to return the oral favor from earlier, she slid down her knees in front of him. Her fingers moved along his thighs, slow and deliberate. His cock was already hard, twitching with anticipation. She licked her lips and smiled. Her small hands wrapped around him, stroking up and down with just enough pressure to make him exhale hard. She flicked her tongue gently over the head, licking up a bead of pre-cum.

"You're gonna ruin me, you know that?" he muttered, already breathless.

She didn't answer with words. Her mouth closed around his tip, tongue swirling.

Chris was turned on by her, and he moaned in delight at her playful teasing. He was glad to have a chance to be with her properly, nothing rushed or driven by unspoken emotions.

Her eyes stayed locked on his, her blue gaze sparkling. She loved watching the tension on his face as she continued to lick him. She placed her mouth over his tip and began to slurp his full girth, bobbing her head, slow at first, then faster with moans of her own. The feeling of his cock filling her mouth was incredible. She loved how he tasted, clean and masculine, with that faint hint of skin-salt that made her mouth water. She wasn't just doing this for him. She enjoyed the way his jaw clenched as she deep-throated him slowly, gagging but not stopping. Drool dripped down her chin, her moans vibrating against his shaft. She could feel her wetness begin to build.

His fingers were wrapped around her hair, pulling lightly, while holding it out of the pool she was dribbling down his rod. Her speed increased as he held her hair out of the way. Her warm, wet mouth felt like heaven.

She couldn't fit all of him into her mouth, but she relaxed her throat as much as possible. As his breathing got quicker, she knew he was about to climax. She wanted him to dump it in her mouth and planned to swallow every bit of him.

"Ahh, Amanda...fuck,!" Chris yelled out.

He tensed, then released. Hot spurts of cum filled her mouth, and she swallowed as much as she could, licking what spilled out the sides. With his fingers still tangled in her hair, he let out another groan.

As she finished and sat up, she kissed the tip one last time, and it sent a shiver through his body. She enjoyed seeing the way he unraveled under her touch, every twitch and moan.

Chris just stared down at her, amazed at what just happened.

"Come up here," he said, pulling her up for a kiss.

They kissed, slow and deep. She climbed on top of him, and they made love. This time, it was slow, tender, full of eye contact and whispers. They moaned together as they both had an orgasm. Afterward, they lay tangled in each other, legs knotted, hearts still racing. Amanda rested her head on his arm and stared at the ceiling, interlacing her hand with his.

So much has changed in this short time. I wonder if he is as happy as I am right now, she thought.

Amanda had always dreamed of these moments. She remembered her teenage years, writing "Amanda Temple," over and over in her notebook. Imagining what it would be like to be his. At twenty-three, she no longer cared who judged her, except her dad.

She drifted to thoughts of Jackson. He was doing much better, but they hadn't really talked since he was released from the hospital. And she had noticed that he and Chris weren't as close either. They would talk over video and the phone, but nothing in person, as far as she knew.

"I wish that—"

"Amanda?" Chris's voice interrupted her.

"Yeah?" she replied, looking towards Chris.

He looked over at her, quiet for a moment because he was trying to think of a way to ask her without sounding soft. But he had to know.

"Remember when LT was in the hospital? You know when you came over here and we had sex for the first time?"

"Of course, I remember silly," said Amanda as she shook her head yes.

"Well, you said...you said that you loved me. Did you mean that?" he whispered to her in a softer voice.

Amanda rolled onto her side and stared at him.

"Absolutely. I love you BT."

The expression on his face looked so serious that she couldn't tell what he was feeling.

"Say it again," he commanded softly.

"I love you, silly man," Amanda said with a huge smile on her face.

Chris blinked, then looked away for a second. The words echoed louder in the quiet than anything he'd ever heard. Inside his chest, they were banging against all the places he thought were non-existent. He swallowed hard, leaned over, and kissed her. He pulled her body on top of him, giving her a long, firm embrace. His hands moved over her body, caressing her curves. As his hands moved, he started to kiss her before his emotions took over.

*****

Outside, Chris sat on his porch smoking a cigarette. He had tried to quit smoking a few times because it was affecting his training, but in recent months, he started back.

He sat there thinking about Amanda. Her beautiful, naked, warm body wrapped in his sheets turned him on. Her blonde hair flowing around his pillow and her perfume floating in the room brought a smile to his face. He could drown in her scent; she smelled divine.

But it was the conversation in bed that had his mind now reeling. She said she loved him.

My entire life, I can't remember anyone speaking those words and meaning it. She seemed like she meant it, but maybe it was just too much emotion for the moment. Or...

Chris thought over what she said repeatedly. His mind would not accept the truth before him, but no parent, relative, teacher, or friend had ever said, 'I Love You,' to him and meant it. Throughout Chris's life, he's never kept a girlfriend, just a rotation of women he liked to hook up with. They would shout out things in bed, some sweet, some dirty, but never those words.

"Damn," he thought to himself. His heart fluttered every time he played back what she said to him.

Chris started to let his pride creep back into his mind, feeling like he was a little boy and needed to get a grip of himself. He was no longer ten years old. However, he knew deep down that he loved her too. He was crazy about her, and now he didn't want to be without her. He just had to figure out how to tell Jackson.

*****

Chris and Jackson had not spoken for some time. But one fateful afternoon, Jackson called him over to the house for a meeting.

"Hey, it's me. I need you to come over for a meeting this afternoon, 1400." Jackson said in a blank voice.

"Yeah, sure LT. I'll be over then," Chris responded. "Ohh, how are you—" was all he could get out before the call ended. No friendly banter or jokes like they used to do.

Feeling like the coldness of the call bothered Chris, but he hoped the meeting wasn't about him having to go on an operation. Lately, he was trying to spend every moment with Amanda.

When Chris reached Jackson's house, he couldn't help but smile at the thought of seeing Amanda's beautiful face. They wouldn't act on their feelings in front of Jackson, but at least they got to see each other. It had been three days since they last spent time with each other.

When he rang the doorbell, Amanda ran to answer. She wore a spaghetti-strap, light pink summer dress that stopped mid-thigh and no shoes, exposing her white toenails.

"Hi BT," she said as she reached out and grabbed his crotch, giving it a light rub.

"Stop that. Are you nuts?" He whispered with a smile and instantly got an erection.

With a sly smile, she called out, "Daddy, BT's here!"

"Tell him to come on up then," he yelled back.

Chris followed closely behind Amanda as they walked to Jackson's study. He grabbed the back of her dress and pulled her towards him. She was so warm pressed up against his chest. She reached for his hands and placed them around her waist.

He leaned in and gave her a quick kiss on the back of her neck. Just as he did, she playfully broke free and ascended the stairs. At the top, she flipped up her dress to reveal no panties, just her beautiful ass. She laughed and went on to her room. Chris took a deep breath and continued to the study, willing his erection away.

Jackson was sitting behind his desk, writing some notes, tilting his glasses up as he was trying to read. Chris stood in the doorway, waiting to be invited in. Jackson looked up and motioned for him to enter. He quickly walked in and sat down.

"Just give me one second, I'm almost done with this paperwork," Jackson said, still looking down.

"No worries, take your time, LT."

Chris began looking around the study. He loved this part of the house. The room rarely changed, but he had changed so much since he first saw it. So many laughs and secret meetings with the unit were hidden in the magical ears of the walls.

Jackson finished his work and leaned up. He took his glasses off while rubbing his eyes. Chris noticed that he looked tired.

"How are you doing, LT?"

"I'm okay. How are you?" he responded.

"Ohh, I'm feeling good. I started a new workout routine. I think going later in the evening works better than mornings for me. Thanks for asking. So, what did you want to see me about?"

Jackson stared at him for a moment without responding. He just shook his head as if he were responding to a question.

"You're feeling great," he repeated. "Hmm, would that have anything to do with you sleeping with my daughter?"

Chris could feel his eyes get bigger. The silence that filled the study was as thick as a brick wall. All the air was seemingly sucked out of the room at that moment. Chris couldn't swallow, move, nor could he answer the question. Both men continued to stare at each other in silence for what seemed like an eternity.

"You know, I've given you access to my house for a long time. When you came here to join the team, I opened my home to you because you seemed like a good guy. But, you've also had access to my daughter all those years as well. My young, naïve, and impressionable daughter. The thought that I trusted you with her makes me fucking sick!" Jackson stated with his last words rising to a yell, with emphasis.

Chris needed to say something, but when he opened his mouth, no words came out.

"No response, huh? Okay, well, let me try. So, how long has this been going on? Since she was fourteen, fifteen, sixteen? Answer me, you sick fuck!" Jackson said without yelling but in an equally quiet, worrisome tone.

"Fuck no, LT! I swear, I never even thought about touching her until after this birthday. She was definitely an adult before anything happened. I never even thought about her like that until recently. I promise you on everything man, I wouldn't do something like that."

Chris was wanting to be anywhere else in the world right now. His face felt hot, he felt thirsty, and his palms started to sweat.

"You know Chris, honestly, I don't know what you would or wouldn't have done. How could you...no, never mind. I don't need an answer to that. I know exactly how you could. I'm aware of Amanda's feelings for you, but I thought you would be a friend, a mature adult, or a good guy and let her down easily. But instead, you let your dick do the thinking." Jackson said in that same quiet tone. "Her being an adult does not matter, and you know that. There is a code; there has always been a code, and you said to hell with that. I'm going balls deep into one of my friend's daughters that I have known since she was a kid."

"Sir, I...," Chris couldn't get out what he wanted to say. He wanted to tell him that he loved Amanda and would do anything to protect her. That he should be happy that they are together.

"Funny thing is...or sad depending on your point of view, others told me it was a big mistake to trust you. That you were just some piece of shit kid from a broken background that would end up disappointing me. I said to them you're wrong. I told them all they were wrong, and that Chris is just a misunderstood guy. Well, looks like the last laugh is on me. Predators groom kids, and just because you waited until she was a 'super adult', that doesn't make it any less vile."

Hearing those words from Jackson made Chris feel like he was kicked in the back of the head with steel boots. The feeling was worse than the day he left his aunt's house. Those particular words coming from his mentor, father figure, and friend hurt him deeply. He felt sick.

"But none of that matters anymore, Chris. So, here is what I want from you," Jackson said, tapping the desk with a finger. "You stay away from my daughter, and you are no longer welcome in this house. She's an adult, but that doesn't mean shit to me. We need to maintain a professional relationship, but aside from that, your connection with this family and friends is done. You hear me, fucking done. Now see yourself out, fucking dirtbag."

With the final emphasis of Jackson's request, Chris got up and slowly walked out of the study. He felt light-headed as he stood up. Chris walked slowly, trying to think, but he couldn't. He was hoping that what just happened was a terrible nightmare.

"This is not happening, how can...I mean we just started seeing each other. She's an adult. She's an adult." Chris just kept repeating that in his mind. He walked down the hall towards the front door. He slowly opened it, turned to look around the house one last time, and then walked out, closing the door as quietly as he could. For almost a decade, this had been his home away from home, his own haven.

Chapter 14

Chris woke to the muffled hum of a car engine, his head pounding like a distant drumbeat. The back seat felt uncomfortably familiar, yet disjointed as if pulled from a half-remembered dream. A sickening churn roiled in his stomach, twisting tighter with each second. His mouth was dry, throat burned. Had he blacked out? Was this the aftermath of something worse? A fight? A night gone sideways? The back seat felt like a coffin lined with confusion. Without thinking, he fumbled for the door handle, shoved it open, and leaned out just in time to empty his gut onto the pavement below.

Chris glanced down and realized he was wearing only a pair of jeans and shoes. His shirt was nowhere in sight. He stumbled out of the car, rubbing his eyes, trying to make sense of his disoriented state and avoid the mound of vomit he just released. The world around him felt familiar, yet it was shrouded in eerie silence and darkness.

In the distance, a faint blue glow caught his attention. Someone was sitting on the steps of a house, their face illuminated by the flickering light of a phone.

"Who the fuck is that?" he wondered, squinting against the darkness.

Chris turned back to his surroundings and spotted his Jeep parked nearby. Relief started to settle in, and when he glanced back at the house, a realization struck like a jolt.

"Seriously? Fuck, I'm an idiot. It's my house," he thought while stumbling across the driveway and up the steps.

Darren put his phone down as Chris approached and sat beside him. Darren passed him a cold bottle of water. He poured some over his head. Then he took a drink before spitting to wash out the taste of vomit. The cold water felt good against his warm body and his still-burning throat. Chris wiped his mouth with the back of his hand. The bitter taste was still clinging to his tongue. His knees ached. His head throbbed like it was caught in a vice. He didn't want to look at Darren, not because he was mad, but because he didn't want to see that look. The one that said, Are you okay? What the fuck man?

"You good?" Darren asked as he patted Chris on the back.

"What, don't I look okay?" Chris said with a weak smile.

"You know I have some questions about tonight, right?" Darren said in a serious tone.

Chris was silent in thought as memories of the night came to the forefront.

"Damn!"

* * * * *

Amanda and Jackson were still not on speaking terms. It had been three weeks since his awkward meeting with Chris. Amanda was excited to see him when Jackson invited him over. She had planned to wait outside for him initially but decided to stay upstairs for a while. After about ten minutes, she heard the door open and close. As she walked to the window, she saw Chris quickly going to his Jeep and speeding off.

Jackson appeared in Amanda's doorway several minutes later, his face a storm of frustration and resolve. He leaned against the frame, his arms crossed tightly.

"Listen," he said in a tone calm but edged with steel. "I know you're an adult, but as long as you live under this roof, you will not see that man."

Amanda's heart sank. For a moment, her voice caught in her throat. She hated disappointing him. But this wasn't about curfews or grades anymore. It was about who she wanted to be—with or without his approval. She straightened her spine, meeting his gaze with defiance.

"You can't tell me who I can and cannot see," she shot back. "Like you just said—I'm an adult."

Jackson's eyes narrowed, his voice sharpening. "That may be true, but I pay your bills. I provide everything you have. Plus, I'm not just telling you—I'm asking you, one adult parent to one adult child: Do not see that man."

Amanda's composure wavered as the words struck her like a hammer. She tried to blink away the tears gathering in her eyes, but they spilled over, tracing silent paths down her cheeks. Her chest tightened as Jackson's ultimatum sank in. He was forcing her to make an impossible choice: her father or the man she loved.

For days, the house became a battlefield of unspoken tension and heated arguments. Jackson laid out his reasons numerous times with growing desperation: Chris had too many demons, too much baggage, he was too old for her, too damaged, and wasn't good enough. But Amanda refused to yield. Every word Branson spoke only solidified her resolve. It didn't matter what he thought. It didn't matter what Chris had been through. She loved him deeply, irrevocably, and that was the only truth that mattered to her.

Each confrontation left Amanda more drained and torn. The walls of her once-familiar home felt like they were closing in, suffocating her with a choice she never wanted to make.

One day, she decided to take a break from everything and spend the day with Lori, enjoying a day of relaxation.

"Lori, hey. Do you want to go shopping and shit today?"

"Yeah sure. I'll be over in a few."

Lori pulled up in her neon green Honda Civic that she calls Slime Time. She laid on the horn for a few seconds while sitting in the driveway. Jackson walked out to the porch and said, "Quit blasting that horn before I come rip it out," with a smile on his face.

"Yes Sir, Captain," Lori replied with a laugh.

"Hey, hey, hey... that's Lieutenant young lady."

They laughed, but both of their faces fell to neutral as Amanda emerged from the doorway. She gave her dad a quick look as she continued down the steps. She hopped in the car. Lori gave Jackson a wave goodbye, and they drove away with some rock music blasting. Amanda didn't look back.

They made their way down GA-400 through the heavy traffic, finally arriving at Phipps Plaza. Phipps wasn't just a mall—it was an escape. A place where the noise of other people's lives could drown out the confusion of her own. As Lori pulled into a parking space, Amanda said, "Wow. I think Slime Time is out of place here."

"Hey, these people wish they had the nerve to drive a car like my Slime. They're just scared," Lori said with a laugh as she rolled up the windows, suppressing the new rock song they played on repeat.

As they stepped out of the car, they checked their outfits in the side mirrors. Amanda was wearing a ribbed white knit tee, a maroon Houndstooth bodycon skirt, and a pair of LeBron 20 sneakers. Lori wore a leopard print bodysuit, cut-off denim shorts, small gold hoop earrings, and a white pair of Vans.

As they walked through Phipps Plaza, about an hour into their journey, Amanda finally decided to discuss the situation.

"I don't know what to do. I love my dad, but this is just too much."

"Yeah, I mean you're grown. Ya know? So, what if your dad's friend likes to cum inside you. That's your business," Lori said with a shrug.

Amanda laughed, but it caught in her chest. The joke was crude-classic Lori, but it dug at something real. Something raw.

"Wow, okay, you are crazy. Always have a way to make me smile. I think I should take a break from him though, just to make sure this is what I want. I mean this is a big deal, because you know how stubborn my dad can be."

"I think that's a good idea. I mean what if you have this problem with your dad and then your relationship with Chris falls apart. What did you go through all the heart break for?" Lori said as she looked at a pair of clear heels.

"I don't know, maybe you're right. I mean things did happen fast, but I know I love him, and he loves me."

"Okay, but are you willing to fuck up your relationship with your dad for it?" Lori asked, looking into Amanda's face.

"I mean don't you think eventually he would come around to the idea? I don't need him to be ecstatic about things, just civil."

"Hey, he's your dad and you know him better than I do, but I think I know guys pretty well. It will take a while for him to be comfortable with this, if ever honestly. He doesn't know that you've had a wet spot for Chris for years, does he?"

"Ohh my god, you're gross," Amanda said with a laugh. "But no, he absolutely doesn't know that. I think that would send him back to the hospital."

"Well, I think maybe just try talking in a calm manner with him. Your dad seems reasonable."

"Sure, he is. Reasonable with things that don't involve me, sure. I don't know, maybe I'll try that. I have to do something," Amanda said as they walked into Build-A-Bear.

Amanda and Lori wandered through the luxurious halls of Phipps Plaza, the high-end stores gleaming under chandeliers that sparkled like starlight. Designer displays showcased the latest fashions and the faint hum of conversation mixed with the rhythmic clicking of shoes on polished marble floors. They moved from store to store, trying on clothes they didn't need and cracking jokes that left them doubled over with laughter.

However, the actions from earlier that morning started to haunt her. Amanda had left her father standing on the porch, his expression a mix of anger and disbelief. She hadn't said a word, hadn't looked back as she slid into Lori's car and slammed the door. She told herself she needed the space, that her father's ultimatum had been unfair. But now, as they sat down for a break near the fountain in the atrium, the memory of his face troubled her.

"Stop looking so serious," Lori said, nudging Amanda with her elbow. "It's a relaxation day, not a therapy session."

Amanda forced a smile, but the guilt lingered. She had walked away without saying she loved him, something she swore to never do again after his heart attack. It was a rash decision, one she hadn't stopped to think through, but the weight of his ultimatum had been too much to bear.

"Should I call and say I love him, but not his stupid rule to not see Chris?"

"I mean, he did have a heart attack and could have died. At least send him a voice message."

"I could text him."

"He is your father, not some random dude you woke up with."

"That is disgusting," Amanda said with a laugh. "Don't ever put father and waking up with in the same sentence again please."

Amanda went to Jackson's contact and sent him a short message: "Sorry about running out and not speaking to you. I love you, but this has been a lot."

She let out a sigh as the 'swoosh' of the sent message played; then they continued with the day.

The spa offered a much-needed distraction. As they reclined in plush chairs, their nails painted in perfect shades of red and gold, and their skin refreshed from a facial series, Amanda finally felt some of her tension ease. She glanced at Lori, who was scrolling through her phone, and let out a sigh.

"Thanks for today. I needed this."

"That's what I'm here for," Lori said with a grin. "Besides, nothing beats pampering here."

By late afternoon, the pair found themselves seated at Davio's Italian Steakhouse. The rich aroma of garlic, butter, and roasted meats surrounded them as they studied the menu. Amanda traced the rim of her water glass, momentarily lost in thought. She kept glancing at her phone, half hoping it would buzz, half terrified that it wouldn't. What if he was regretting everything? What if he'd given up?

Then it buzzed. Chris's name flashed on the screen—BT—and her stomach fluttered.

Lori raised an eyebrow, "Let me guess it's Chris, texting to see if you're mad, or if he can come over and suck on your wet spot?"

Amanda's face flushed crimson, and she let out a surprised laugh. "Lori!" she hissed, though she couldn't keep the smile off her face.

"What?" Lori said, feigning innocence. "You know I'm right."

Amanda rolled her eyes, shaking her head as she picked up the phone. "You're the worst," she muttered, though her tone was light.

"I know, but you love me for it," Lori joked, taking a sip of her drink.

Amanda focused on the lines on her screen.

"Hey beautiful, how's your day going?" Chris typed.

She smiled and replied, "It's going great, just spending time with Lori. How's your day?"

"Well, it's a much better day now. I wish I was there with you."

They continued to text each other, and Amanda felt a sense of comfort knowing that Chris was there for her, even if he wasn't physically with her at that moment.

A few hours later, the hum of Slime Time's engine filled the silence as Amanda stared out the window. The streets of Atlanta were bathed in the warm glow of the setting sun. Lori tapped her fingers on the steering wheel, sneaking glances at Amanda every few seconds.

"You're awfully quiet over there," Lori said, breaking the silence. "Thinking about your dad?"

Amanda sighed, crossing her arms. "I just... I know he's going to be waiting for me, and it's going to be this whole thing. I can already hear the lecture." She mimicked a deep voice. "'As long as you live under my roof...'"

Lori snorted. "Parents are weird like that. They think they're protecting you, but half the time they're just projecting their own fears. I mean, look at my mom. She still calls me every time it rains to make sure I have an umbrella. Like I'm incapable of surviving precipitation."

Amanda chuckled softly. "That's actually kind of sweet."

"Sweetly annoying," Lori corrected. "But seriously, you're going to be fine. And hey, if all else fails, you can always come stay with me. My couch is super comfy. Plus, I've got wine."

Amanda smirked. "Tempting. I'll keep that in mind. I appreciate you so much."

"Duh. You're stuck with me." Lori gave her a sideways grin as they turned onto Amanda's street. "Now, let's see what kind of mood King Branson is in tonight."

"It's not funny, Lori. He's not just mad, he's genuinely hurt. And I get it, but—" she trailed off, shaking her head. "I can't let him dictate my life."

"You're right, it's not funny," Lori said, nodding. "He had a chance to make his own bad decisions, and now it's your turn."

Amanda laughed despite herself. "Chris isn't a bad decision."

Lori shot her a look. "Babe, the man has more baggage than a Delta terminal. I'm just saying, maybe your dad has a point. But!" She held up a finger before Amanda could interrupt. "That doesn't mean he gets to run your life. You're a grown woman. If you want to ride the throbbing Chris train, baggage and all, that's your call."

Amanda rolled her eyes. "Thanks for the pep talk... I think?"

"Anytime," Lori said with a chuckle.

The car slowed, and Amanda's chest tightened as her house came into view, the porch light casting a familiar glow. The warmth of the evening felt cooler now, the air thicker.

Lori parked in the driveway and glanced at her. "You sure you're ready for this?"

"Nope," Amanda said, gripping the door handle. "But I'm doing it anyway."

"Atta girl," Lori said as she gave Amanda a hug.

"Well, thanks for everything today. I really needed that to clear my head."

"Hey, of course what are friends for. Just take it easy on your dad okay. He might surprise you."

"Okay, well text me when you get home."

"I will."

Amanda got out of the car and walked up to her front door as Lori drove off into the coming darkness. She opened the door, but to her surprise, Jackson was nowhere to be found.

"Dad?" she called softly, hoping he'd answer. The silence was deafening. It was the kind that made her wonder if she'd already lost something she couldn't get back. Still, she was relieved that she wouldn't have to talk to him just yet. She went to her room and texted Chris, "I'm home. I miss you."

He replied, "I'll be heading home soon. I miss you too. We'll get through this together."

Amanda smiled at the message lighting up her screen. Things could work out after all. She knew it wouldn't be easy but was willing to fight for their relationship.

Chapter 15

One thought, "Damn!"

It echoed like a bullet ricocheting in his skull. Not just recent events but everything. Losing control. Losing Jackson. Almost losing Amanda. His stomach turned again, this time from shame more than booze.

That was all Chris could think, sitting on the steps, remembering the night with Darren.

The evening at Bar Margot with Darren started out well. The bar sits at one of the highest points in downtown Alpharetta, and it skillfully merges the distinction between inside and outside in a vibrant setting, with Kennesaw Mountain in the distance.

Chris sat with Darren, nursing a scotch cocktail, while he was texting Amanda. He was happy to be messaging her, but he was also trying to distract himself from the messy situation. He knew how much she was struggling with her dad's disapproval of their relationship and wished he could do more to help her.

Darren noticed Chris's distracted demeanor and asked, "What's on your mind, man? I mean here we are with this badass view and all the pussy you could want, but you're sitting here all mopey and shit."

Chris sighed and took another sip of his drink.

"Well, I need to tell you something man, but I don't want you to freak out, cool?"

"Yeah dude, you can tell me whatever, unless it's some shit about you being in love with me. Then we might have a problem." Darren said with a heavy laugh.

"Ha, nah man nothing like that. It's about Amanda."

"You mean like Branson? Amanda Branson?"

"Yeah, her. LT and I had a serious conversation that... well, didn't make anyone happy."

"Dude, are you trying to tell me that you and Amanda are bumping uglies?"

"Well, that crude description would be correct, yeah. Her dad found out and is giving her a hard time about us being together. I mean he straight up told me that I was expelled from the 'family,' but I don't care about me. I hate seeing her so upset."

Darren nodded sympathetically as he listened to Chris, the pain in his friend's voice seeping through.

"Ohh, umm, yeah that's tough. But you know, this is something that you just can't rush. Sometimes you have to let people figure things out in their own time. You can't force someone to accept something they're not ready for, ya know?"

"Yeah, but what if he's never ready man?" Chris asked as he chugged the rest of his drink.

"Well, in that case, I guess you'll just have to decide if that's something you can live with. I mean at this point LT already told you you're dead to him. So, I guess don't worry about it," Darren said with a shrug of his shoulders.

Chris looked down at his empty glass, not yet responding. Darren called the bartender over and ordered a round of double shots of Jameson.

"Hey, my man. Let me get two doubles down here. My guy got some real shit going on."

The bartender nodded. They sat quietly for a while, waiting for the drinks to come. They soaked in the random chatter and laughter of the other patrons. Finally, their shots arrived, and they took them without saying a word.

Chris stared at the bottom of his glass and finally spoke. "LT used to keep a stash of good whiskey in his study. Every time I passed an eval, he'd pour me two fingers, toast to my growth, say I was like a son to him." He swallowed hard. "Now he looks at me like I'm nothing. Like I betrayed him. Yeah, he said I'm not a part of the family anymore, or some shit like that, it hurt man. I mean they both have been the closest thing to family for me. On top of it all, I just can't believe that he would think I'd groom Amanda during that time. I never saw her that way! She was the one that made me see it, but it wasn't until she was an adult, fuck man." Chris said as he ordered another round.

"I hear you bro, but it is his daughter. I'm not saying that he's right and you groomed her or whatever, but even as an adult, he still feels the need to protect his child. I'm no expert by any means because I don't have kids, but I don't know how I would react. Plus, it could be that he just needs time to see his daughter for the wonderful woman that she is, and not some little girl anymore."

"I hope you're right man. I want to be with her, but I don't want her to cut her dad off and then resent me later. That is a terrible feeling."

Darren sat quietly for a minute, contemplating the statement. "I hadn't thought of it from that point of view. It would be a big burden to have that weight on your relationship, huh."

"We are texting each other, so that's something. I'm trying to give it distance and time, but it's hard not seeing her."

Chris's phone buzzed. Amanda sent a heart emoji along with "Thinking about you." He smiled, but it didn't reach his eyes. He was thinking about her, too. Every second. She didn't deserve this kind of pressure. Not from him. Not from her dad. Not from anyone.

"Yeah but just try to let LT come around in his own time. You know how that fucker can be."

Chris knew Darren was right, but it didn't make the situation any easier. He took the next shot and said, "Thanks for the advice. I just hope it works out for us. I feel like I'm putting her in a rough spot. A new relationship with me, but she can't be happy because for the first time in her life, her dad's disappointed in her and that's tough."

Darren put a hand on Chris's shoulder to reassure his friend.

"You know I've got your back brother."

They sat in silence for a few moments, sipping their new drinks. Then Darren spoke up.

"Hey, what happened with you and that April chick? Does she still call you?"

"Ohh, nice change of subject there," Chris said with a laugh. "Yeah, she texted me like an hour ago, asking if we could talk. I don't have anything to say to her though."

"Hmm... does she know about you an Amanda?"

"Hell nah. If she knew that she would probably try to cause some trouble. I think she just needs to move on. There was nothing serious between us anyway."

Darren shrugged. "Yeah, you probably right about that. Well, do you care if I give her a call?"

"Yeah... wait what? You want to talk to her?" Chris said with a chuckle.

"I mean, if you don't care, and she's available. I mean she is hot." Darren said with hope in his voice.

"Hey dude, if you don't care that I've been with her, then I don't care. I have feelings for Amanda, not April. Plus, there was this whole situation at my house before."

"What happened?" Darren asked, leaning into the conversation.

"Well... I don't want to go into the whole thing, but needless to say I know who I want."

"Cool brother. Let me get her number. I'll shoot her a message to let her know that you good with me dumping some loads in her. See if we can get something going. "

"Wow! How respectful of you."

"Hey, I'm just being honest. I'll ask her first, but if that hot ass woman lets me, I'm dropping loads all inside her." Darren said with a laugh.

Chris smiled, "Thanks, Darren. You always know how to put things in perspective."

"That's what I'm fuckin' here for man. Now let's drink to better and more sex filled days ahead."

They clinked their glasses together and took a long swig of their drinks.

As the night grew longer, the multiple cocktails, beers, and Jameson shots started to take their toll on Chris's distracted mind. The more he drank, the worse he felt. Feeling tortured and confrontational. Who the fuck does LT think he is? This is not a mission, and I don't have to listen to him. I will not turn my back on her, and we will not hide our relationship. Chris wasn't just drinking; he was unraveling. His limbs were heavy, voice slurred, eyes glassy. But in his chest, that fire still burned. Guilt. Rage. Grief. And under all of it, love.

"Fuck it," he muttered. Chris's mind kept going, and he decided to see Amanda right then.

"Hey, will you drive me to LT's place? I want to see her right now."

Darren looked confused. "Umm... how about fuck and no. First of all, you're drunk as shit. Second, I'm just as drunk as you. Plus, are you insane? You know he doesn't want you to be at the house. Just text her and tell her to meet us here."

"No, I don't want to run from this. I think if the three of us sit down and talk, we can come up with something," Chris said, slurring his words.

"Yeah, well the answer is no. Let's just get a ride and go home."

Chris, clearly not happy with that response, grabbed his keys off the bar and started to walk towards the door. Darren quickly jumped from his seat to follow him.

"Hey brother, what the fuck are you doing? You're way too drunk to drive man."

"I'll be alright. I'll open the windows and play Hootie and the Blowfish."

"Nah, man, stop. You might kill someone or yourself. You need..." was all Darren could get out before Chris slipped out the door, hopped into his Jeep, and sped off.

Chris slowed his speed and finally put on his seatbelt as he got onto the highway. The road warped under his headlights, bending like waves. Hootie played on the speakers, but the words twisted and slurred into background noise. He let the breeze slap his face, hoping it would sober him up.

He could imagine her now, laughing in his passenger seat, legs up on the dash, eyes sparkling. I love you, BT. He needed that voice right now.

Ignoring the risks of driving in his inebriated state, he decided that seeing Amanda was worth the risk. She was his only family now that Jackson had disowned him. Hearing those words from Jackson hurt him deeply. Chris continued to go over things in his head as he cruised down the highway, with the crisp and moist evening air caressing his face and head. The smell of flowers in the air and lights of the city were equally intoxicating. His music choice had him singing along with some of Hootie's most energetic songs.

Chris finally made it to the house. He pulled into the Lieutenant's driveway and sat there for a minute, deciding if he should go to the door. It had been hours since his last text exchange with Amanda. He wondered if she was sleeping.

Jackson was relaxing in his study when he heard the Jeep pull into the driveway. He had a gut feeling it was Chris and hoped that he wouldn't cause a scene at his house.

It had been a long time since Chris had gotten this drunk.

Chris thought to himself, sitting in the Jeep, "Never has a woman done this to me. Amanda is my woman, and I'm going to fight for her."

He slowly made his way out of the driver's seat, almost falling to the ground, and walked to the steps. Not so gracefully, he ascended the steps and stood toes to the front door. He banged on the door three times. No one answered. As he raised his hand to pound on the door again, it slowly began to open. Standing in the doorway facing Chris was Jackson Branson. He was wearing his black cotton robe and reading glasses, with his face sporting a frown.

"Chris, go home son," he said to him in a smooth tone.

"No. I need to speak with the two of you right fucking now!" Chris slurred with some spit landing on Jackson's robe.

Jackson felt some patience was necessary because Chris was oozing alcohol. His eyes were red, his clothes disheveled, and he was swaying. As he started to close the door, Chris stuck his foot in the threshold and kneed it back open.

Jackson's eyes widened. "Chris take your ass home now, before you get yourself in a world of hurt!" Jackson said in a much louder tone.

Chris shook his head no. He looked over Jackson's shoulder, down the hallway, to see if Amanda was there. He saw no signs of her and returned his gaze to Jackson.

"If you don't want anything to do with me, then that's fine. I hate it, but it's fine. But fuck you, LT, if you think I'm going to let you ruin what could be a special relationship. Don't you see what you're doing is wrong? Making her choose is not right." Chris said with angry, slurred words.

"And you'll do what exactly, if I don't move out of your way so you can date my daughter that you've known since she was a child?"

Chris looked around again, ignoring the question.

"Amanda!" he shouted at the top of his lungs.

"She's not here," Jackson answered.

"Well, where is she?" Chris asked. "She fuckin said she was here."

"You take your drunk ass home now," Jackson said as he slammed the door in Chris's face.

Just as Jackson slammed the door in his face, Darren pulled into the driveway. He jumped out of his car and heard Chris yelling at the closed door.

"Where the fuck is she?!" he screamed as he kicked the door. "Ten fucking years and you want to kick me out of your home like I'm trash. You try and keep her away from me and I will fuck up your life you piece of shit!"

Darren ran up to the door and tried to calm Chris down.

"Come on, brother, let it go," he said, trying to convince Chris to leave before things escalated.

Chris jerked his arm away and started kicking the door again.

"Fuck this guy. Open the door you son of a bitch!"

"Jesus, BT come on. Let's go, fuck!" was all Darren could say.

"Goddamn it. Amanda, I can't stop thinking about you. I hate the way things are right now, but I'm willing to fight for you." Chris shouted with the left side of his face pressed against the dew-covered door.

Meanwhile, inside, Jackson let out another sigh as he debated what he should do. He didn't want to do it, but he grabbed his phone and told Siri to call Patrol. He thought that by turning Chris over to them, he could have some pull and would ask them to go easy on him. Despite everything that was happening, he didn't want this personal situation to derail Chris's career. At this point, Jackson was sure Chris had woken up half of the neighborhood.

When they first crossed paths all those years ago, Jackson noticed that Chris often struggled to rein in his feelings. He knew that if things didn't change tonight, Chris would keep going until he got himself in serious trouble.

While on the phone, Jackson could hear Chris's muffled voice arguing with Darren and rambling about family.

"You don't want me as a part of your family anymore, huh? What kind of man with honor does that?" Chris screamed, leaning against the door. His chest now heaving from his rage, sweat rolling down his forehead.

"Yo, BT get a fucking grip!" Darren yelled as he wrapped his hands around Chris's waist and pulled him away from the door. The brief struggle ripped Chris's shirt.

"Where the fuck is she?" Chris tried to yell, but it came out as more of a hoarse whisper. Suddenly, he felt weak and light-headed. The alcohol, mixed with anger and a lack of sleep, started to slow him down.

Patrol showed up shortly after Chris began to calm down. Officers Enes and Jones pulled Chris away from Darren and cuffed his hands in front of him. Chris felt his insides begin to churn. He leaned over and vomited on the lawn as the officers were walking him to the car.

"Ugh, well that tastes wonderful," Chris said with a laugh as he described the chunkiness of his vomit pile. "Hey, is that the potato I ate earlier?"

The officers didn't respond. They got to the car, opened the door, and Chris calmly got in. Once they had him securely in the car, the officers walked back to the house to speak with Jackson. He emerged from the house and checked the door for damage. There were a few smudges and scrapes, but overall, it was still in good shape.

"Hey, Lieutenant Branson, we're sorry this is happening, Sir. We tried to get here quickly, but there was a huge wreck on GA-400. What would you like us to do with him? Maybe spend the night in holding?" Officer Enes asked.

"I mean, whatever you can do to keep him from getting a record. He just needs to sleep it off somewhere else. Plus, I'm fine, no harm done. Well, other than some scuffs to the door," Jackson answered while looking at the door. "I just don't want him to harm someone or himself."

As Jackson was finishing his sentence, there was a loud crash of glass. They all looked toward the patrol car and saw the window shattered. Darren and the officers ran towards the car.

"You idiot! Chris, you need to chill out man."

"That piece of shit," Enes's voice trailed off as he ran towards the car.

The right-side window was completely gone. There was glass scattered on the driveway. The shards were emblematic of Chris's psyche tonight. As Jones and Enes approached the vehicle, Jackson called out to them.

"Hey, wait a minute. Can you uncuff him please? I will pay for the window as long as this stays between us, okay?" said Jackson.

Enes gave Jackson a bewildered look. "Sir, this guy might be your friend or whatever, but he needs to go to jail. I don't trust leaving him here."

"No, no. He won't stay here. I'll take him home if someone can help me get him in the car," Darren interjected.

"Alright guys, fine. Me and Jones will follow you to his place to make sure he goes home. But if we have to come back, he will go to jail."

"Thank you. He just has a lot going on, and this is his rock bottom day of letting all his feelings out." Darren said with a somber tone.

"Well, we're not therapists, so get your guy some help." Jones said as they got Chris out of the car and uncuffed him.

Finally, Darren and the officers were able to coax Chris into Darren's car.

Sitting in the car, Chris looked his friend in the eyes and said, "I really fucked up tonight, didn't I?" Darren silently put the car in reverse, turned his head to back out of the driveway, and left.

Jackson shook the officer's hands. "Thank you for showing some restraint."

"This is all the leeway he is going to get. He may have things going on but being shit faced and making a scene is not okay." Jones replied.

"I know. I know. Let me put my boots on then we can head to his place and drop off his Jeep."

Jackson slowly walked back into the house to put on his boots. The external lights were still illuminating the night ambiance of the yard. He got the boots on and slowly rubbed his hands together. The smell of the night air resonated with him as he thanked God that he didn't have hurt Chris.

Chapter 16

Chris wondered what his plan was and, furthermore, what he'd hoped to accomplish by going to Jackson's house. He kept replaying the moment he shouted at Jackson, the look of disappointment in the man's eyes. It had burned deeper than any scolding ever could.

He was thoroughly confused by his actions. He didn't mean to kick out the patrol car window, but he began feeling claustrophobic at that moment, in the car. As they sat on the steps of his house, he stared out at nothing, lost in thought. Mindlessly swatting at mosquitoes.

He thought back to his life with his aunt and uncle, Sybil and Harold. When he was around seven or eight, he got his first 'punishment' for doing something bad. He forgot to put his clean clothes in the dresser and left them in the laundry basket. Harold decided to lock him in the linen closet for several hours. It was small and dark with thin shelves. The overpowering smell of detergent and bleach made his head hurt. Chris squeezed himself underneath the lowest shelf, covered his face with his shirt, and lay there in the fetal position. He thought he was going to die. He couldn't catch his breath as the strong linen scent of the dryer sheets mixed with the lint on the floor made breathing more difficult. The fear of death he felt at that moment was overwhelming for his young mind. But he survived. And as the abuse continued, he learned ways to keep himself amused while locked in the closet.

Randomly, thoughts of his own personal hell, being in that dark room, would encroach on his happy thoughts. His throat tightened like he was back in that closet like the walls were shrinking again.

Chris shook the traumatic memory from his mind and came back to current events. But it still sat on his chest like a cinder block. He was about to stand up when Darren pulled him back down.

"So, can I say something without you getting mad?" Darren asked.

Chris shook his head yes as he rubbed his eyes. He hoped it wasn't something that would make his head throb worse.

"You are a decent-looking dude, so I hear, and there are lots of women that would line up to fuck you. So why in all of the world would you dick down the Lieutenant's daughter?" Darren asked, looking at his friend.

Chris sat there for a moment, pondering the question. He wanted to be mad, but he couldn't. The question hit too close to a truth he hadn't been ready to face. He didn't plan to fall for her. He just did.

"I don't know man. Honestly, I tried to stay away from her, but it didn't work."

"Well then, may I suggest that you try harder!" Darren said with a yell.

"Damn man don't yell. My head feels like someone is prying it apart with a crowbar. Why should I when my heart telling me I want to be with her."

"You mean your dick is telling you to be with her."

Chris turned toward Darren. "Yo, fuck you! It's not even like that with us."

"But you knew that she's LT's daughter! Why couldn't you just stay away from her?" Darren said as he stood up and walked down the steps. He looked at Chris, eye level. "We grew up with her like she was our little sister. Those corny ass parties and all. Yeah, sure, she's an adult and sexy as hell, but there's somethings that guys just shouldn't do."

"Just drop it, okay?" Chris said as he felt anger start to build.

"No, I'm not going to drop it. For once in your life, you need to listen to reason. I thought you said they were like family. What kind of inbred family did you have in mind?"

Chris sighed loudly, "Hey don't start talking shit man. I'm not in the mood for this shit. I feel awful already. I loved them and I was so grateful to have them in my life."

Darren laughed, shaking his head, "Well, you sure got a weird ass way of showing your appreciation. Spraying cum in his daughter."

The words hit Chris like a slap, and he stood up. His hands were curled into fists, jaw flexed, and vision tunneling. But just as he started to walk down the steps, Darren backed away.

"Hey man, sorry about that last one. That was in bad taste, but you get what I mean right? All I'm saying is that we knew her from a young age, and she grew in front of us. She might be an adult now, but LT is her father. All he can see is some guy that may have been ogling his young daughter, just waiting for the right moment to pounce."

"Yeah, well you know me better than that. I don't know man; I just don't know." Chris said as he slowly sat down on the bottom step.

"Well look, don't stay out here, go in the house, stay there, and get some rest okay?"

Chris stared at the gravel under his feet, the quiet night pressing on him. Every mistake, every word spoken, seemed to echo louder under the moonlight. He didn't know if he was the villain or just broken.

"Yeah, you're probably right. Thanks for helping man. And quit talking so much shit. I was ready fuck you up." Chris said with a slight smile.

"Yeah sure. You could've tried. Hit me up later man, and don't do anything else stupid." Darren said as he gave his friend a fist bump and left.

Chris took a deep breath and heaved his body into the house. He made it to the couch and plopped down. The scent of Amanda made his thoughts race as he passed out. In the darkness, he didn't notice the letter that was left at his door.

* * * * *

Somewhere else, under the same sky, Amanda sat with a pen in hand and her heart full of guilt. The words she couldn't say aloud began to pour onto the paper. Once done, she sealed the envelope and made her way over to Chris's house to leave it, just as he decided to visit that night.

♡ The Heart of the Matter ♡

As one chapter ends, and the paramours part,
Under the night glow, of the third rocks art,
Their hearts entwined, yet still they yearn,
For the troubles of love, they must learn.
In the hush of the night,
Within the evenings tender light,
Two souls echo in unity,
Chained by love's melancholy melody.
A murmur in the breeze, as thoughts lament,
A yearning gaze given, time not spent,
The chapter concludes, yet a love persists,
In every plane, every joy, even in the abyss.
In quietude of the closed gentle sigh,
Beneath this moon's gentle sunny eye,
The tale of love that slowly spins,
A fresh chapter hesitantly begins.

BT, as I sit here writing you this poem, I think I fucked up. I should have talked with my dad before anything happened with us. Just to let him know, you aren't some creep, but that I really have feelings for you. That I wanted you first. I don't know, I figured writing some poetry would help me clear my mind. I hope I get to see you at the ball in a few weeks.

I miss you.

Chapter 17

Amanda scanned the ballroom, looking for Chris. For weeks, communication between her and Chris had slowed to almost nothing after she left her letter at his house. She didn't understand why he changed so much; the letter was supposed to reassure him, not scare him away. They hadn't even talked on the phone. She was hoping that Chris would show up to the ball.

Her palms were already clammy. She'd reapplied her lip gloss twice and checked the door every thirty seconds. The silence between them these past weeks had been deafening, and now it felt like everything was riding on this one night, the AVG Ball.

The AVG Ball is a yearly celebration for the veterans in the city provided by the Atlanta Valor Gala Foundation. It was a star-studded event, with prominent people from across the state attending, including many of the professional athletes in the city.

As she made her way through the room, she greeted many people she hadn't seen since the previous year. Many superficial pleasantries were exchanged as she slowly moved towards the open bar. She was wearing a black, sleek gown with a thigh-high slit up the side. Her four-inch open-toed heels were peeking through the slit displaying her fresh pedicure. Her hair was full of life, with her blonde curls projecting volume. Finally, she reached the bar and asked for a glass of white wine.

Amanda took a slow sip as she watched the door, waiting for Chris to show up. Then, after roughly thirty minutes, she saw his amazing, chiseled frame come through the door, and time slowed. His suit hugged every inch of muscle memory she'd tried to forget, and his presence hit her like gravity. Her breath caught, her heart raced. She got lost in her feelings as she watched him walk through the room.

"Damn he looks amazing," she thought as she got another glass of wine. Chris made his way over to Jackson.

"Hello, Sir. Long time no see," Chris said with a smile.

"Hello, Mr. Temple," Jackson replied with a cold blank stare. He hadn't referred to him as Mr. Temple in years. "I don't expect that we will have any unpleasantness like at my house a few weeks ago, correct?"

"Uhh, no sir. Nothing like that. I think that we should sit down and talk about everything, actually. It took some time, but I've given things some serious thought."

"Well, Mr. Temple, I don't think we have anything to discuss, but I'm open for adult dialogue if you're able to control yourself. And you know what I mean by control yourself." Jackson said with an emphasis.

"Okay, great to hear, Sir. I will reach out to you soon." Chris said as he smiled and walked towards the bar.

As he approached the bar, he saw Amanda standing there sipping her wine. She was staring at him, watching him walk across the large room. Once he got to the bar, he ordered two drinks, one scotch on the rocks and some tequila specialty drink the mixologist created. The order confused Amanda, as she knew that Chris didn't usually drink tequila. She walked around the people between them and came up behind him. She was about to tap him on the shoulder, but someone else spoke first.

"Hey, you. About time you showed up," said a redheaded woman wearing a silver mini-dress. She put her right hand in the middle of Chris's back as she took the drink from him with her left.

"Rachel! Hey, I was wondering where you were. I was just going to hang onto your drink until you showed up. How long have you been here?" Chris said, looking down at the redhead. He could feel Amanda staring at him from the side, but he didn't look in her direction.

The smile had left Amanda's face. She couldn't be seeing this right. This had to be a friend, cousin, sister, or something. But her wonder was corrected when Chris leaned down and kissed Rachel on the lips. Amanda felt like she was going to throw up. Suddenly, it got hot and humid in the room. She felt like screaming and attacking them both. But she composed herself and hurried towards the bathroom.

"Hey what's wrong," her dad asked as she walked past him.

"Take a look over there. That's what. I bet you're fucking happy now." She said as she continued to the bathroom.

Jackson looked over and saw Chris lean down to kiss Rachel again.

"Ohh, that's why he wants to talk to me. Good, the dirtbag is learning," Jackson thought as he returned his conversation with Bill, one of the foundation's board members.

Amanda's chest tightened with every step. The music blurred into static. All the weeks of waiting, hoping, and second-guessing were unraveling faster than she could breathe.

In the bathroom, Amanda looked in the mirror as tears stung her eyes. She barely made it before the tears came.

She was mumbling to herself. "So, this is why he hasn't been talking to me. He's moved on already. All this time fighting with my father and for what? For him to just fuck some other bitch."

*****

Rachel looked at Chris and said, "When are you going to ask me to dance?"

"I don't know. I'm not really in a dancing mood right now."

"You're normally fun, but tonight you're being weird. What's going on? I mean you invited me to this ball. Did you not want me to come?" Rachel said with annoyance in her voice.

"It's nothing, really. I think I just need another drink. You know, I need to loosen up."

Rachel pulled his head close to her and licked the bottom of his ear, then whispered, "Maybe you just need to treat me like a drink and put me in your mouth."

She smiled at him, and his demeanor changed. Chris grabbed Rachel's hand and led her out to the dance floor. He grabbed a handful of Rachel's ass as she started to grind into him, rubbing her hands on his body while singing off-key to the song.

*****

In the bathroom, Amanda heard the bass drop of her favorite song, Simmer Down by Donnay.

Usually, she would have been happy and on the floor dancing, but she was distraught and in the bathroom alone. She dabbed at the corner of her eyes and leaned against the tile wall. The coolness from the wall slowed her racing mind.

As she was deciding how to apologize to her father, a familiar deep voice broke her thinking. "You look beautiful."

Amanda opened her eyes and looked up to meet Chris's gaze.

"What do you want?" she asked in a cold tone.

"I just came to see how you were doing. You ran off when you saw me kiss Rachel, and I was just checking on you."

"How I'm doing? I left that letter at your house, and you disappear. I figured, maybe you just needed time to see things from a new perspective. But you just needed time to find someone else to fuck."

"It wasn't like that at all. After that night at your house, I didn't know what to do. I care about you, but the thought of making a woman chose me over her father just doesn't sit right. The letter made me feel that more. I was just trying to do the right thing here."

"Chris, I love my dad more than anything, but I am an adult. My relationship with him should have nothing to do with you."

"Amanda, I get that, I really do. But you have to understand from my point of view, too. You guys were the first real family I've had. He is your dad, but he was also the closest thing I've had to a dad. Without him, who knows what my life would be right now."

"Well, I can see that your life right now includes a redhead in a short skirt. Fuck you, BT." Amanda said as she turned to walk out of the bathroom.

"Anytime, anyplace," Chris replied as he grabbed her arm, slowing her walk.

The two exchanged a look. A look that began to melt Amanda's resolve.

She tossed the tissue away and turned to look in the mirror at Chris. He stepped closer to Amanda and stood behind her.

The air between them pulsed with heat. His reflection hovered behind hers, eyes dark, jaw tense. A man pulled between restraint and desire. Every inch of space between them felt like temptation.

He got a chill thinking of what happened the last time they were in the bathroom together.

"So, are you saying you want to show me a good time tonight?" he whispered to her.

Her heart was pounding. Part rage, part heartbreak, part pent-up heat. She didn't know if she wanted to cry, scream, or fuck him into oblivion.

Amanda turned quickly and slapped him with all the force she had in her body. Chris was silent, in shock from the slap. Amanda raised her hand to hit him again, but he grabbed her wrist and pushed her away. She stumbled back and caught herself with the hand dryer.

"What the fuck do you think you're doing? You hit me."

"I know I hit you. I wanted to hit you twice. Why didn't you at least tell me what you were thinking? Is a text from you too much to ask. I left that letter, and nothing. Not even a message, email, DM, nothing. I got not one damn thing from you. Then, you show up here with Roshel." Amanda said, now almost screaming.

"Don't do that again. I don't hit you and expect the same respect. And her name is Rachel. I don't know why I stopped talking to you. I just can't think when it comes to you. The way I feel about you is new to me. I know you might be spoiled, but you can't snap your little fingers and get me to act how you want."

"I might be spoiled, but I still treat people with dignity, unlike you."

"Dignity, I damn near got arrested for your ass. I wanted everyone to sit down and talk like we used to do. So, tell me what doing the right thing has gotten me?" Chris yelled.

"You what?" Amanda asked. "Arrested, when was this?"

"A few weeks ago, when I came over to your house to talk. The same night you dropped that letter off." Chris said, his hands becoming more animated as he spoke.

Jackson hadn't mentioned anything to Amanda about Chris coming over and banging on the door. She asked about the glass in the driveway, but Jackson made up a story.

"So, you came by the house then?"

Her mind spun. All this time, she thought he ignored her out of cowardice, but it was mainly because he'd fucked up. It didn't excuse everything, but it rewrote the story she'd been telling herself.

"You mean LT didn't tell you?

"No, he didn't tell me shit."

"Okay, well, quick version. I got shit faced with Darren at the bar, told him about everything, and then decided I wanted the three of us to talk. So, I drove, when I shouldn't have, and got your house. I banged on the door and made a real scene out there. LT told me you were out, maybe on a date or something, and I lost it. He called Patrol, and I might have slightly kicked their window out. They let me go home though, so no jail." Chris said with increased breathing from the quick explanation.

Amanda stood in silence for a second, then banging on the bathroom door broke her trance. Chris had locked the door when he came in, and the line outside was growing. She was processing this new information but was still confused by his actions.

"Okay, even with all that, who is that woman you're with?"

"Literally, no one gives a shit. She was just, there I guess."

"I care, BT. I care," she replied.

"I get that. She was just around to help me try and move on. She knows that it's not serious. That's all I mean."

Amanda reached up and wrapped her arms around Chris's neck. In an instant, he lifted her off the floor and pushed her into the wall. Both of his hands were cupping her thighs. Chris felt his insides burning for her. He didn't know how she did it to him, but it didn't matter. The animalistic attraction was undeniable.

She couldn't quite put her finger on it. Was it the way he gazed at her, the gentle strength of his grip, or the intensity radiating from him? Whatever it was, a warm thrill began to grow within her. She could sense the delightful wetness stirring between her legs.

"Don't you want to slide inside me?" she asked in a sultry voice.

"Amanda, don't fuck with me. You know I would love that," he whispered back.

But, the overpowering excitement had left him, and reason came back to his mind. He lowered her to the floor, then stepped toward the door.

"You know," he said while in deep thought. "I believed you when you told me you loved me. I still do."

"BT, I—" Amanda started.

"Don't worry about it. Right now isn't the right time. Give me a call later, maybe," Chris said to her as he unlocked the door and walked out, past two women giving him a scowl.

One of the women, Janet Graves, walked in and saw a flustered Amanda. Janet was an old friend of the family but was not up to date on the current situation.

"Hey, you okay Mandy?" she said in a comforting voice.

"Shit, I'm sorry. I'm a mess right now. We...I mean I didn't mean to take so long." Amanda said as she fanned her face, trying to ignore her hot flushed cheeks. Even her chest was beet red.

"No problem. But, umm... do you think it's wise to have an encounter with so many people around?"

"Ohh, no. It was not that. We were just talking."

"That must have been one hell of a conversation then." Janet replied with a smile. "Wasn't that Jackson's friend Chris?"

Amanda mumbled, "Yes."

"Girl, you are something else. I'm not here to judge, but you're something else. Don't get hurt climbing that mountain of a man." Janet laughed as she went into the stall.

"It's not like that. It's...well, complicated."

"Hey, none of my business. I've just heard that he can be a little crazy, and I want you to be safe. And I mean, safe," Janet said, peeking through the crack of the stall door.

Amanda didn't respond at first. She was just thinking of his hardened body on top of her, and it made the moisture overflow.

"Well, I will see you out there," Amanda finally replied.

"Absolutely! And hey, I didn't mean to butt in on your thing like that. I just saw him and thought it was an intriguing scene. Anyway, I'll catch you out there, Mandy," Janet replied with an audible smile.

Amanda checked her face and walked out of the bathroom.

The music was loud, and there were many more people now. She was wading through the sea of people when someone grabbed her arm. The person pulled her backward toward the back of the room. She was about to fight back, but then she noticed it was Chris. As they got to the back of the room, he put his strong arms around her waist and directed her to a hallway that would lead them to the front of the building.

"What are you doing? Are we really sneaking out right now?" Amanda asked with amusement.

"I'm doing what I have to do." Chris replied. "Just trust me, okay."

Amanda followed Chris quietly to the valet stand.

"Leaving early, Sir? You planning on coming back?" asked the valet.

"Yeah, getting out of here. Nah, man we not coming back." Chris replied.

When they brought Chris's Jeep around, he opened the door for Amanda. They hadn't said a word to each other. She pulled her dress up slightly and got in. He ran around the Jeep and sprang into the driver's seat, leaned over, and kissed her.

The soft, tender kiss quickly turned into something deeper, more desperate. Chris's hand slid to the back of Amanda's neck, his fingers threading through her hair as he pulled her closer. A quiet sigh escaped her lips as she melted into him, her body tilting toward his, her dress inching higher as she shifted in the seat. Amanda's fingers brushed against his jaw, her touch light yet deliberate. His other hand found her thigh, gripping it just enough to make her breath hitch. The heat between them was undeniable, searing through the small space of the Jeep. When they finally broke apart, Amanda's lips were parted, her chest rising and falling with each unsteady breath. Chris rested his forehead against hers for a lingering second before he pulled away. "Put on your seatbelt," he finally spoke.

"I got it," she replied with a smirk.

Chris put the Jeep in drive, and the engine growled to life as they eased into the Atlanta night. Amanda leaned back in the passenger seat, her lips still tingling from the kiss, her breath uneven as she stared out the windshield. Chris's hand remained on her thigh, warm and firm, not moving. Just holding her there like he couldn't bear to let go.

"I missed this," she whispered.

Chris glanced over, "You missed me."

She smiled, turning her head toward him. "Yeah, but I missed us."

The silence between them stretched, but it wasn't uncomfortable. It was thick with heat, tension, and possibility. For the first time in weeks, neither of them felt like running.

"Whatever this is, we take it slow. We do it right. You with me?" Chris said over the engine.

Amanda reached across and laced her fingers with his.

"Ride or die," she said, her voice low and certain.

"Well hopefully not die, but I get it," Chris said with a chuckle.

"Ohh, ha, ha, you know what I mean," Amanda said as she glared at the side of Chris's face.

As the Jeep roared into the night, it held two souls tangled in something messy, hot, and absolutely worth the fight.

Author's Note

Whew, you made it to the end.

Heat & Honor is a steamy, emotionally raw series where the lines between duty, desire, and devotion blur. These stories are messy, taboo, a little toxic, and hot.

I wouldn't have it any other way.

Stay tuned for the next book in the ***Heat & Honor*** series.

Did you like it?

Leave a review.

Tell your friends. Tell your therapist. Hell, tell your sneaky friend if they've got a thing for forbidden drama and bodies against walls.

Thanks for rolling in the fire with me.

See you in the next round of bad ideas.

— *[Chad Wannamaker]*

www.ingramcontent.com/pod-product-compliance
Lightning Source LLC
La Vergne TN
LVHW090610110826
845146LV00001B/329

* 9 7 9 8 9 9 5 4 9 8 6 1 2 *